THE SHADOW OF VALKO

The Valko Kid felt one of the posse's bullets ripping through his flesh. Wounded, he managed to ride on, with only willpower keeping him in his saddle. But he is confronted by a female sheriff and collapses at her feet. Slung into jail, Valko hears the sound of a gallows being hastily erected in his honour. Then in rides the impostor who has caused him to be branded an outlaw — and Valko manages to salvage his reputation and mete out deadly justice.

Books by Michael D. George
in the Linford Western Library:

MICHAEL D. GEORGE

THE SHADOW OF VALKO

Complete and Unabridged

LINFORD
Leicester

First published in Great Britain in 2000 by
Robert Hale Limited
London

First Linford Edition
published 2002
by arrangement with
Robert Hale Limited
London

British Library CIP Data

George, Michael D.
    The shadow of Valko.—Large print ed.—
Linford western library
1. Western stories
2. Large type books
I. Title
823.9'14 [F]

ISBN 0–7089–9821–6

Published by
F. A. Thorpe (Publishing)
Anstey, Leicestershire

Set by Words & Graphics Ltd.
Anstey, Leicestershire
Printed and bound in Great Britain by
T. J. International Ltd., Padstow, Cornwall

This book is printed on acid-free paper

Dedicated to the Duke

Prologue

The outlaw known simply as the Valko Kid seemed to be in the most serious of situations. Never far ahead of an ensuing posse, he rode on and on trying to clear his name. It had become a vain venture of late. Knowing you are innocent was little comfort to the rider of the magnificent white stallion. The Valko Kid's only salvation was to find the true culprit who had lived in his shadow and prove his own innocence.

As hard as he tried to find the man who hid behind black clothing and rode a pale dapple-grey horse, Valko failed. His every effort seemed cursed by the dogged determination of one man who led the posse. Marshal Clem Everett would not give up his relentless pursuit of the young outlaw. His was a quest which took on almost biblical proportions. Everett would not quit, it was not his way.

Valko continually sought clues to where he ought to ride in order to detect the ruthless pretender who had ruined his life and branded his name into infamy. Yet the Kid never seemed able to go more than a few days before the posse caught up with him again and forced him to flee once more.

It had become little more than an existence where once there had been a life. Only the thought of one day catching the man who had ruined everything he had once held dear, gave Valko the strength to continue.

Days had turned into weeks which in turn had become years and still Valko was no closer to the man he sought. Somewhere out there the animal who wore black and rode a similar horse to his own continued his path of destruction. If Valko had time to think he might have already encountered the bandit yet there was never any time. With each passing day it seemed his reputation and value Dead or Alive grew.

The last time he had managed to shake off the posse for a matter of only a few short days he had ridden into a small town called Indian Ridge and found himself embroiled in trouble. Valko had managed to find a few days of peace in Indian Ridge, and also a brief moment of romance with a demure café owner named Mary White. Somehow she had managed to penetrate his defences and it had been his only moment of happiness since he had first found himself wrongly branded as an outlaw.

Had he been anyone else he might have allowed himself to remain with the beautiful Mary, but the Valko Kid knew there was little option but to saddle up his faithful stallion and continue his quest.

For a brief while Valko thought he had picked up the scent of the ruthless killer who used his identity to such catastrophic effect but then it happened again: Marshal Clem Everett and his posse suddenly appeared as if from nowhere and forced the young outlaw to desperately escape their rain of bullets. Now he had no choice but to ride fast and hard for his life. No longer able to track the true villain who continually added one vicious act upon another, the Valko Kid had little option but to try and outride the blazing guns behind him.

Guns which for the first time had managed to find their mark.

Now wounded, only the power of his ageing mount kept his neck from being stretched by the inexorable posse.

1

The Valko Kid had never seen a sky more black nor filled with as many stars. Yet for all its splendour, there seemed to be a warning written in the universe above his head. The outlaw had ridden a hundred miles into the heart of a land he neither knew nor recognized.

He had ridden hard, not through choice but through necessity. When you could smell the men who wanted to collect the reward on your head, you just kept riding.

Giving the last of his canteen's precious water to Snow, his gallant white stallion, the tall man clad all in black stood silently squinting at the strange landscape before him.

This place was like the absent face of the moon. Devoid of anything remotely welcoming. Even at night, this place echoed its deadly danger.

The Valko Kid was weary yet knew there was no time to rest for him. Not here. Not here amid the flat prairie with nothing taller than sagebrush to hide behind. The shapes of mountains could be clearly seen as they cut across the black star-filled sky, but how far away were they?

Valko knew the mountains offered his only salvation but how long would it take for him to reach them, and was it possible to find a route to safety through their majestic spires?

Even darkness offered no protection for the man who had long ridden the range trying to keep one step ahead of the posse which never gave up its chase. A wanted man because of his being mistaken for a ruthless killer, the Valko Kid had no time to rest. One day he prayed the truth would become known and his name would be cleared. One day, he might find the man who had stolen more than just his name.

Holding on to the saddle horn he

rested his fevered brow against the cool worn silver livery and sighed heavily. Pain now dominated his every moment. Sleep was but a distant memory. For three days and nights they had been on his trail, relentless in the pursuit of their prey. Valko had become confused. For weeks he had been free and for the hundredth time thought he was safe. Then the posse had appeared once more as if from nowhere.

Whether it was the same posse which had dogged his trail for the previous year was not clear. All the outlaw knew was they were keen. The bullet hole in his shoulder was proof of that.

Whoever had shot him was good with a long rifle. The first day the posse had appeared he had barely had time to mount Snow when he felt the crippling agony tearing through his shoulder. The bullet had passed straight through but left a legacy of burning flesh which had yet to cease its torture.

Now he had to keep riding.

Somewhere out there in the darkness

7

behind him Valko could hear the thunderous sound of hooves charging toward him. Being afraid of something he could not see was a new experience for the wounded outlaw as he hauled himself back into the saddle. Gathering up the long leather reins, he somehow managed to get the horse moving again.

Snow began to gallop as Valko held tightly on to the reins and leaned down over the saddle horn. The mountains before them appeared to get no closer — however hard the faithful steed charged. They were beaten and worn yet it was not in their nature to quit until life itself finally escaped their grasp.

For another two hours the horse somehow galloped at a speed which only a magnificent thoroughbred could maintain.

Mile after mile, Snow continued. It was as if the huge animal knew its master was closer to violent death than he had ever been before. Mile after mile the white stallion thundered across the frost-covered ground toward the mountain range. Somehow the outlaw hung on to consciousness, as his faithful horse valiantly tried to increase the distance between himself and their pursuers.

Finally finding himself able to sit upright, Valko gritted his teeth and narrowed his eyes.

The first rays of sun began to trace across the prairie allowing Valko to see the mountains were now within his reach.

Turning to look over his shoulder he could see the dust of the posse a dozen miles behind him. It had to be Marshal Clem Everett leading the posse, Valko concluded. Only his tenacity could have kept the band of deputies on his trail for so long.

Reining in, Valko desperately looked for a place to hide, which might just allow him time to recover. Somewhere to water and feed Snow. As hard as he looked, his tired eyes could see no safe haven.

★ ★ ★

'There he is, boys,' the grim-featured Marshal Clem Everett exclaimed loudly from atop his lathered chestnut. 'I reckon we could catch him within the hour.'

'We are sure gaining on the varmint, Clem,' the burly Josh Cavey snarled, as the group of ten riders drew level with one another.

'He's carrying my lead,' Booth Dawson laughed, rubbing the spit from his mouth. 'I told ya all I winged him.'

Everett knew any normal man would order his men to rest themselves and their horses but he was no normal man. He was driven by something deep within his craw which never allowed him to rest. He had chased this outlaw too far and for too long.

Now he could smell the stale sweat of his prey on the morning air as the stars succumbed to the warming glow of daybreak.

'We gotta keep going,' Everett drooled.

'I figure we will have the critter in range soon and then we can finish him.'

'But I thought you wanted to take him alive, Clem?' Josh Cavey said.

'It's taken too damn long, boys. Valko ain't no normal man and I figure if we wanna catch him we gotta shoot him off that stallion.' Everett gave a long stare around the faces of his men.

There was a hushed silence as the men gathered their rigging together and spurred their mounts on once more.

This was a group of men with one purpose: they had to kill the fleeing outlaw because it was the only way of ever stopping him.

* * *

Leading the big white stallion through the tall brush, Valko used every ounce of his cunning to seek a trail which might give him at least a chance of escaping the posse.

The brush was dry even though covered with the frost of night as the

11

outlaw made his way through it. The pebbles beneath his high heeled boots were smooth and appeared to have once been a river bed. Yet there was no sign of water now.

Looking up, the mountains loomed over him. Valko felt uneasy as he tried vainly to find a place to rest. He knew with every passing second the men on his trail grew closer.

He had perhaps an hour before they were upon him. If he was lucky they would not lynch him on the spot although the trees before him would prove mighty tempting to any posse.

Had he ridden into a place where there was no escape?

Was this how it would end, for the Valko Kid?

His right arm ached as he led Snow on. The bullet hole no longer bled but it filled his every thought as it sent burning messages through his weary body.

The trees were sparse and thin on the edge of the prairie but grew stronger and thicker the closer he got to the mountains.

Then he felt Snow pulling back on the reins and snorting as if trying to tell his master something. Valko stopped and looked back at the creature who was nodding excitedly up and down. The white mane seemed to float in the thin air as the outlaw ran his hand over its neck.

'What's wrong, Snow?'

Releasing the reins, he watched as the horse reared up on to his back legs and kicked out at the sky.

Following the trotting stallion, Valko soon discovered what his four-legged friend had sensed. A thin bubbling creek seemed to be coming out of the rocky ground and then disappearing again a mere six feet away.

Valko watched in amazement as the horse began drinking as he caught up with it.

Taking the canteen from the saddle horn, the outlaw knelt down and began filling it with the crystal-clear water.

Valko wondered how many times had his bacon been saved by the old stallion.

The voice which filled his ears was cool, soft and definitely female.

'Easy, stranger,' it said in a warm yet tough husky tone.

Valko slowly turned his head and stared at the long barrel of the rifle aimed at him before focusing on the tall slim female who wore a star on her heavy coat.

'Ma'am?' His tired voice echoed his confusion at the strange sight.

'Get up and keep both hands on that canteen, mister,' she ordered.

The Valko Kid got to his feet and stood holding the canteen as he had been instructed.

'You a sheriff?'

Striding towards him she seemed angry at the question which he had posed.

'You got a problem with that, mister?' she spat.

'I reckon not, ma'am.' Valko felt his

14

head spinning as he replied. 'I just never seen a girl wearing a star before.'

'I'm a sheriff all right, mister.'

'Best-looking law officer I ever seen.'

'You look kinda familiar, mister,' she noted. 'You wanted for something?'

'Maybe.' Valko inhaled deeply.

'I reckon you're an outlaw.' She cocked the Winchester eagerly.

'I'd be a liar if I denied it, ma'am.' Valko suddenly felt giddy and stumbled backward. Unable to maintain his balance, he fell at the feet of his white horse.

Cautiously, the female moved towards the stricken outlaw keeping a bead on him. If he had never seen a woman wearing a star before, she had never seen a fully grown man faint.

Kicking him several times with a silver-tipped boot, she concluded he was genuinely unconscious. Then her attractive eyes saw the wound in his right shoulder.

★ ★ ★

The town was large by any standards a man cared to use. Yet up in the narrow mountain pass it was almost a miracle. Gold had built this town in a valley perched between two enormous peaks and although the pickings were now harder to find, it still thrived. Expertly, the female sheriff steered her mount up to the hitching rail with the larger white stallion in tow. The streets were empty at this hour as she dismounted to survey her trophy.

As Valko's face was slapped enough times to bruise his cheeks he managed to awaken. She had tied his hands and somehow managed to hoist him over the saddle of his stallion. His eyes opened and looked down at the ground and the strange view of his horse's hooves and left stirrup. It took a while for the outlaw to realize he was lying on his belly over the saddle and was tied on good and tight.

Then he saw her silver-tipped boots coming into his limited field of view.

'So you're awake?' Her voice was

16

mellow like melted chocolate and even though she had hurt him, he somehow could not find it in himself to get angry.

'Yep,' he answered, wondering how long she would force him to remain lying over his saddle.

'Reckon you must be worth a few dollars.'

'A few,' Valko admitted, as he watched her feet disappearing around the front of Snow.

'What they call you, mister?'

'Valko.'

'The Valko Kid?' There was a note of surprise in her voice as her fingers untied the rope which had held him secure during the long steep climb to this strange place.

'Yep. They call me the Valko Kid.'

'You got a few nasty wrinkles there for a man called 'kid'.'

'Life ain't been kind, ma'am.' Valko felt strangely refreshed after sleeping with his head dangling next to his stirrup.

'How much you got on your head,

Valko?' She tossed the rope over the horse and he watched it hit the dirt.

'Too much.'

'I got me a mess of brand new Wanted posters in the office, Valko.' She pulled him down on to his feet and allowed him to get his wind back.

'You gonna claim the reward money, ma'am?' His face looked pale as he managed to stand upright beside her.

'Reckon so.'

The long pistol encouraged him to step up on to the boardwalk and enter the large and well-constructed sheriff's office. He paused for a moment and stared down at his hands, which were bound tightly.

'You tie a good knot, ma'am.'

'Get into the cell, Valko.' She waved her gun at him as he dragged his tired legs into the awaiting cell.

He listened to the key rotating in its lock before turning to face her.

'You gonna untie my hands, ma'am?'

'When I'm good and ready.' She walked to her desk and opened the top

18

drawer. He watched her pull out a pile of Wanted posters and start to flick her way through them. Then she stopped and raised both her eyebrows.

'How much am I worth now?' he queried.

'Twenty-five thousand dollars.'

'It's gone up,' he sighed.

'Dead or alive,' she chuckled.

Sitting on the cot he blew out heavily. 'No wonder I got wrinkles.'

Her face darted up and she stared hard at him.

'You ain't got too many wrinkles, Valko.' She smiled.

'I ain't?'

'Nope. You ain't,' she confirmed.

★　★　★

The posse had made slow time getting across the wide prairie. A mixture of weary riders and spent horses had made Marshal Clem Everett regret his decision to continue without allowing them to rest.

How Valko's stallion had managed to increase the distance between them was a mystery to the hard lawman. Yet if any horse could manage to gallop after three days of constant riding it had to be the white stallion.

The group of men were now near the mountains and searching through the vast tree-covered slopes. Not for the outlaw but for water. Their canteens were dry and so were they.

'We lost him, Clem?' the gritty Booth Dawson asked as they all trudged through the trees seeking a stream or pond to fill their canteens.

'He ain't far,' Everett drawled.

'He ain't here,' Cavey chipped in.

'He's carrying lead,' Everett smiled. 'I figure he's close.'

The ten men fanned out until they located the small creek and then converged upon it. They made camp and built a large fire.

'Valko is probably lying dead somewhere close,' Dawson grinned.

Everett placed the large blackened

coffee pot into the flames before sitting next to his horse.

'Valko don't die so easy, boys.'

'At least we can get some hot grub into our guts,' Cavey declared as he dropped his saddlebags next to the fire. 'Valko has to eat jerky.'

Everett thought hard as his men went about their business of making themselves a hot meal. Yet again the Valko Kid had disappeared as if swallowed by the earth itself. This time though, Everett was determined to find him.

This time he would kill him.

2

Doc Jenkins was a man who had seen more in his sixty years than he cared to recall. It had been a life trimmed with happiness and grief. Both in equal measure had been poured into the cup of his life; wagon trains of brutality and joy; the results of Indian attacks and the carnage spilled through revenge. This was a man with tired eyes and hair the same colour as Valko's horse. He had been in this remote township since it first saw a canvas tent being erected. He had grown wealthy because of the miners who paid for everything in gold ore. His had been a life of tending the sick and burying the dead. He had brought people into the world and seen as many depart. Jenks was his name to all who had ever known him yet he was not what he appeared to be.

There had been a time four decades

earlier when he had been more than a mere doctor, more than a man who cared for the sick. His life had once travelled the same route as Valko's. Then he had not been known as Doc Jenkins or Jenks. Then he had been called Ralph Hanks.

Good fortune had spared him the life of the hunted outlaw and he had earned his right to be respected, but 'way deep within him, a memory lingered, the memory of what once had been; the remembrance of a life he had so luckily managed to escape.

As his frail hand turned the door handle of the sheriff's office, he felt his heart skip a beat. This was like travelling back to a time in his life he had tried to forget for over forty years.

The Valko Kid looked up at the man who entered the office holding his small black medical bag. Valko stood and moved to the bars of the cell he had found himself caged in. His hands were still bound as the female gazed up from her chair and smiled at the old man.

'Jenks,' she said fondly.

'I got your message, Bet.' The man frowned.

'Sorry to wake you.'

'I was awake.' Jenks seemed nervous as he moved to the desk keeping his back to the outlaw. 'What do you want me to do?'

'I've got me a real valuable bandit there.' The female stood and pointed at the cells.

'So?'

'He's wounded,' she added.

Jenks reluctantly followed her to the iron bars where Valko stood silently.

'Who is he?'

'My names Valko,' the Kid said quickly.

'The Valko Kid.' Jenks looked at the tall man who stood square-jawed before him. His were the eyes of a man who had once been an outlaw.

'You the doctor?' Valko asked.

'Y . . . yes,' Jenks replied.

'Got me a hole in my shoulder.' Valko pointed his nose to his right shoulder.

The female pushed the large key into the lock and turned it until the bolt released. Valko stepped back and watched as she covered the elderly man with her trusty pistol.

Jenks entered and looked the man up and down.

'You'll have to cut these bindings off his wrists, Bet,' Jenks said thoughtfully. 'I can't tend his shoulder with his hands tied like this.'

For a moment she hesitated. 'You sure, Jenks?'

'Positive, Bet.' The old man waited as she pulled a long knife from her belt and moved closer to the tall outlaw.

'Hold your hands out, Valko,' she ordered waving her gun in one hand whilst gripping the six-inch blade in the other. 'I'll plug you if you make a wrong move.'

Valko held his hands out and watched as the razor-sharp blade slid through the bindings. For the first time in hours he could feel the blood rushing to his fingers once more.

'What they call you, ma'am?'

'Sheriff,' she snapped stepping back out of the cell with her gun trained on him.

Jenks moved Valko to the cot and sat him down.

'Better remove your shirt, son.'

Valko fumbled with his buttons before pulling off the shirt to reveal the wound.

'Is it bad?'

'I've seen worse.' Jenks moved from the front of the Kid's shoulder to the back.

'What's wrong, Jenks?' she asked.

'This man was shot in the back,' the medical man observed, shaking his head in disgust.

Her face went sallow. 'You were shot in the back, Valko?'

'Yep.'

'That sure is a yellow-belly thing to do.'

Jenks looked at her. 'Even to an outlaw.'

'Right enough.' She moved so she could see the wound more clearly.

'Get me some boiling water, Bet,' the doctor ordered.

'What for?' She raised her eyebrows. 'I hope he ain't having a baby too.'

'This wound is infected.' Jenks opened his bag and searched for a scalpel. 'I've gotta cut him deep to clean out the poison.'

She edged toward the stove before turning.

'Hell, I can't cover you and boil water at the same time, Jenks.'

'Betty Jones,' Jenks snapped, 'I will not come to any harm with this prisoner.'

'How can you be so sure?'

'I can tell.' Jenks rested a hand upon Valko's back.

Shrugging, the sheriff holstered her gun and proceeded to prepare the stove to boil up some water.

The Valko Kid sat passively watching her before casting a glance at the elderly man.

'How can you tell I'm trustworthy, Jenks?'

Jenks patted the outlaw's back. 'I can tell.'

Valko felt the scalpel tracing the wound in his shoulder.

'So her name's Betty Jones, huh?'

'Be careful, Valko. She's as dangerous as a diamond back.'

'I ain't ever been snake bit, Jenks,' Valko grinned as the pain raced through him.

'She ain't ever taken a prisoner before,' Jenks sighed.

'How come?'

'She usually brings them in dead.'

Valko felt his throat tighten as he swallowed.

★   ★   ★

'What do they call this town, Jenks?' Valko asked as he felt the poison seeping down his back as the doctor cleaned the bullet entry hole in his right shoulder-blade.

'Bear Claw,' the old man replied whilst using his vast experience at tending wounds in order to get every last trace of poison out of the deep bullet hole.

Screwing his eyes. Valko gritted his teeth. 'Bear Claw you say?'

'Yep. Bear Claw.' Finally the probing and cutting ceased and Jenks dipped a rag in a bottle of iodine before pushing it into the hole in Valko's back.

The outlaw arched his torso and made a grunting noise as the burning sensation ripped through him. It had been only a matter of months since he had been shot before in the small township of Indian Ridge, a town where he had left more than his blood, where he had loved someone for the first and perhaps only time.

'Oh my,' he blurted at the ceiling.

'Hurt?' Betty Jones asked from behind the desk where she had taken refuge when Jenks had started to get serious about his unpleasant chore. She had seen a lot of blood in her time but there was something about seeing a surgeon's lance probing into the flesh of a person which turned her guts.

Valko shook his head. 'Yep. It hurts, Sheriff. It hurts real bad.'

'You must be a real well-brought-up *hombre*, Valko.' Jenks placed a loose bandage over the wound and taped it to the pale flesh.

'How do you figure that, Jenks?' Valko asked, as he watched the old man move to the exit wound below his right collar bone.

'You never cursed.' Jenks wiped the flesh with the iodine before satisfying himself his job was done.

'Oh I cursed,' Valko smiled.

'Inside?'

'Yep. Inside, Jenks.' The outlaw bent forward and shook his head as if trying to recover from the previous hour's constant carving up of his flesh. He felt better for all the pain he had endured. The steady throbbing of the wound had ceased and now only stinging remained.

The Valko Kid could handle stinging.

'This scar?' Jenks ran his finger across the barely healed wound which traced the outlaw's ribs. 'It has only just healed and you've been shot again.'

'Back shot twice in a matter of weeks,' Valko laughed.

'How long have you been running, Valko?' Jenks frowned as he stared hard into the face of the young man.

'Too damn long, Jenks.' The face seemed empty of anything resembling hope.

'How did you become an outlaw?' the doctor queried.

'Maybe I never did.' Valko shook his head as he studied the floor between his boots.

'I don't understand.'

'You and me both, Jenks.' The smile was hollow. A gesture to someone he felt at ease with.

'He fit enough for me to shoot, Jenks?' Betty asked the old man who was rolling his sleeves back down.

The look upon the old wrinkled face gave her cause to smile.

'Shoot him?'

'He's wanted dead or alive according to this poster.' The face of the female gave little away. Both men assumed she was joking, but neither would have bet money on it.

'She as hard as she sounds, Jenks?' Valko cast a glance up at the old man who was now putting his dark frockcoat back on.

'Definitely, my boy,' Jenks nodded as he walked out of the cell carrying his small medical bag.

The sheriff rose to her feet and moved around to the doctor as he dusted off his sleeves in turn.

'I imagine I shall not get paid for this, Bet?' Jenks did not need the money but he often felt it would be nice to be offered some from the town elders.

'Ask the mayor.' She lifted the heavy keys off her desk and moved to the cells. For a brief moment she hesitated as she looked at the handsome profile of her prisoner. His dark hair hung over his face as he rested. It was a good face, she found herself thinking. Not the face of a man who was reported to have done so many evil things.

Placing the key into the lock she pushed the cell door shut before turning it. The sound of the bolt engaging caused the half-naked man to turn and stare up at her from his bunk.

He smiled and she hurriedly turned away.

'Is he fit now, Jenks?' she asked in a loud embarrassed fashion.

'He's as good as new.' Jenks picked up his hat from her desk and carefully placed it on to his head. 'I reckon he ought to rest for a few days though.'

'That's fine.' She moved to the window and stared out at the street which was beginning to come to life.

Jenks lifted up the Wanted poster and read all the details attributed to her prisoner before rubbing his chin with a nicotine-stained thumb.

After a moment, the attractive female looked across into his tired old eyes and sighed. 'I know what you're thinking, Jenks.'

'You do?'

'The description don't fit him.'

'But he admits he is the Valko Kid, Bet.'

Her face seemed troubled. 'And this sheet of paper states the Valko Kid is a down-and-out filthy killer. I find it hard to believe he did half of what's written down here.'

Jenks stared across at her prisoner before turning the door handle and stepping out on to the boardwalk.

'Jenks.' Her voice made the man pause.

'I do not understand it either, Bet.' He shook his head. 'I will tell you one thing though . . . '

'What?'

'That young man is not a cold-blooded killer. How on earth he has become wanted is a question I'd like to delve into with him later.' Jenks tipped his hat and closed the office door behind him before taking in a lungful of the fresh morning air.

Betty Jones placed her blue-denimed rear on the edge of her desk as she watched the old doctor walking down the long quiet street and thought. According to the poster she had captured one of the most dangerous evil creatures who roamed the West. That was what the poster said. A man who was worth $25,000. Yet since encountering the outlaw she had seen nothing to justify any of the claims. The man in her cell was softly spoken and polite. He had the nature of a preacher, not an outlaw, but he admitted he was the infamous Valko. Why?

Could the poster be wrong?

Could he be acting?

Even the Valko Kid could not possibly be capable of changing from a black-hearted desperado into this quiet man, she thought.

The harder she pondered the questions, the more confused she became. If he was dangerous, surely it did not show. Toying with his fancy shooting rig which lay across her desk, she wondered why Jenks had not been alarmed by the man. How he had willingly placed himself in danger. Jenks had seen a lot more of life than she, and he seemed to share her doubts.

Why had he been so honest and even gone as far as to tell her his name and not deny he was a wanted outlaw?

He could have lied.

Why did he choose to tell the truth?

Gazing up she looked at his handsome features as he simply sat on the cot in his cell. He had no anger nor venom. Betty Jones ran her fingernails over her tin sheriff's star and sighed.

Whoever the Valko Kid was, he was a puzzlement.

3

Bear Claw was a town of more than thirty saloons. Each and every one of them had done a brisk trade since the humble beginnings of this strange mountain settlement. The gold diggings were now quieter than they had once been, but there was still enough ore and dust to sprinkle over the various businesses and keep them thriving.

Bear Claw stood in the high valley between two massive tree-covered mountain peaks. It was high enough to be elusive to most of the happenings which cursed the West, yet a vital route from one land to another. Settlers had travelled from distant less friendly places hoping they might discover another world where their sort might just have a chance.

Wagon trains had found this place and used it constantly as a valuable time-saving trail to places offering more fertile land and a chance of finding a future devoid of the pain behind them.

Some unhitched their wagons when they arrived in Bear Claw and stayed. Others came and left as quickly as possible. Bear Claw was not a town which appealed to everyone.

Indians too had travelled peacefully between the two unnamed peaks. Fewer with each passing season, they were now more of a memory than a regular sight.

Bear Claw had survived where other gold towns had withered and crumbled into the dirt from whence they had sprouted. Here, there seemed to be a genuine life and comradeship few other towns could equal. The buildings were not just wooden structures, but built to last from stone and red brick. Here, prosperity had long overtaken the fragile roots of a place built on gold nuggets. Here, the people had gelled into a real community. Thirty saloon and dance halls provided vital entertainment for the hundreds of miners who lived in and around the settlement. The hundreds of good-time girls who plied their trade lived well and only age caused retirement from this most profitable of places.

This was a town known to those who used the trail taking people to better more exotic places. It lived off those people and provided something far more valuable than mere provisions to the weary wagon masters. Bear Claw had it all and more.

The town had seen it all during its brief existence, but it had never had a notorious outlaw caged within the four walls of its sheriff's office. Until today.

Bear Claw had a mayor and town council and almost everything civilization required of a modern town, but it still hung on to its frontier mentality, clinging desperately to its unique and vital sense of what it was and had always been. Bear Claw had no churches nor places where the religious might take refuge, but it had families who somehow lived shoulder to shoulder with all the rougher elements of a town which was still, and had always been, a boom town.

The news of Sheriff Betty Jones's latest prisoner spread quickly through the buildings as life began to stir within the confines of the town.

A mixture of curiosity and out and out nosiness seemed to overwhelm the citizens of Bear Claw. Mostly females of a certain age and profession came to try and spy through the windows of the sheriff's office although Betty Jones soon drew down the green shades. It was not the sight of these scanty dresses which upset the tough attractive sheriff but the fact she felt a strange need to protect her prisoner.

By the time the large town hall clock had struck ten that morning, it seemed every living breathing man woman and child knew the Valko Kid was in her cell and had joined the females outside the office.

By the time the large minute hand of the clock had reached the expertly painted six upon its dial, the building had more than 200 souls standing before it.

None angry, all curious.

At ten minutes to eleven the mayor and a half dozen of his council members were marching down the long sidewalk in a hurried procession towards the sheriff's office.

Monte Scott was no mere professional politician even though he was a twice elected mayor. Money spoke in this strange township and Scott had the loudest voice of all.

His were the roots of a man who had managed to make the grade against all the odds. Since drifting into Bear Claw countless years earlier, Scott had soon found it easier to claim the vast virgin forests which dominated the two mountain peaks and use the lumber than dig for the elusive golden ore. Monte Scott had seen the possibilities of trees and the wealth they would provide for a man smart enough to fell them for the vast Eastern market.

Over the years, lumber had made him richer than any of the area's gold miners. They had become wealthy and then for the most part, seen their life's labours dissolve into distant memories whilst Monte Scott continued to get richer and richer.

The crowd parted as the officials approached the sheriff's office with Scott at their head.

Sheriff Betty Jones's eyes flashed up as the troop of men followed Monte Scott into her sacred office. For a brief moment the sound of the crowd outside could be heard buzzing as they managed to get a glimpse of her prisoner through the half-open door. As it was closed once more, the sound of the excited townspeople became indistinct.

She had never been impressed by either Scott or any of his flunkies and seeing them barging into her domain made her not inconsiderable chest measurements swell with fury.

'Well?' she asked the large well-heeled man and his followers.

Scott was silent as he strode across the floor toward the caged outlaw with his less important entourage in tow.

The sheriff rose from her chair and moved to the cell where the seven men stood studying her valuable prisoner.

'What do you want, Mr Mayor?' she asked.

'I take it this creature is the Valko Kid?' Scott rubbed his neck as if unable to work out if the man seated was truly as notorious as his reputation implied.

'This is Valko.' Betty Jones edged around the men and stared hard into their faces.

Valko had not moved from his cot since Jenks had departed and seemed uninterested by their attention. His eyes gazed at the floor as if unwilling to acknowledge their presence.

'So you are the infamous Valko Kid?' Scott boomed down at the outlaw who still sat as the doctor had left him.

Valko continued staring at the floor silently.

'Is he deaf?' one of the men asked.

'Nope. He ain't deaf,' Betty Jones replied.

'Are you the Valko Kid?' Scott shouted at the caged man angrily.

Valko still stared down at the floor without bothering to acknowledge any of the men.

'Why doesn't he reply, Sheriff?' Scott blazed at the female who was now smiling, unable to hide her amusement.

She shrugged. 'He's kinda particular who he confabs with, boys.'

'Good Lord, I demand you make him answer my questions.' Scott had changed colour as he fumed out his words.

'Mr Mayor, I cannot make him answer if he don't wanna answer.' She moved around the men trying not to display her amusement.

'If you were a man . . . ' Scott raged.

'But I ain't a man.' Her voice showed its ability to pitch at his volume.

Scott marched in a circle around the office for a few moments before stopping at her desk and staring at the magnificent gunbelt laid across its top. The guns were unlike any he had ever seen before. They were the rig of a gunfighter.

'Are these his weapons?' Scott slid one of the Colts from its holster and looked at it fondly.

'Yep.' She walked to the desk and took the pistol from the mayor's hands and returned it to its holster.

'An evil shooting rig if ever I saw one,' the big man blurted.

'Fancy, but hardly evil.'

'Why did you bring him here to Bear Claw?' Scott slammed a fist down on to her desk violently.

'What if he has a gang?' Another of the men shuddered.

'Exactly. They might ride in and slaughter innocent women and children just to free their boss,' Scott ranted.

'Valko rides alone,' Betty Jones responded.

The seven men huddled for a moment before the red-faced mayor broke free to confront the sheriff.

'We only let you have this job because your father served Bear Claw so well until his accident, Betty,' Scott hissed.

'The folks of Bear Claw voted me in fair and square, Mr Mayor,' she responded. 'I was duly elected.'

'They felt sorry for you,' Scott snarled.

'I beat your boy by two to one, Mayor.' Betty Jones saw the Valko Kid looking in their direction as she defended herself against the verbal onslaught.

There was a heat within the office which seemed to be fuelled by pure hatred. Its intensity caused the outlaw to slowly rise to his feet. Stepping to the bars of his cell he gripped the cold iron rods and cleared his throat. Each, and every one of the group turned and focused upon him standing proudly before them.

It was Scott who spoke first. 'So now you've decided to speak.'

'Yep,' Valko replied, staring hard at the men.

They approached cautiously, as if fearing the bars of the cell might not restrain him.

'You are the Valko Kid?' Scott asked.

'That's what they call me, Mayor,' the Kid answered slowly.

'Why have you decided to talk now when only a few moments ago you were mute?' the large well-fed man snarled.

Valko pushed the dark hair from his face. 'I don't like gangs of men bullying females.'

'Bullying?'

'Yep. Bullying, Mayor.' Valko rubbed his chin and felt the growth of three days in the saddle respond. 'I don't cotton to folks who try and get rough on no woman. Even if she does wear a star. In my book, that's bullying.'

'We don't need no outlaw to teach us manners,' one of Scott's men said.

Valko narrowed his eyes.

'Only a coward hassles a female.'

'I don't need your help, Valko.' Betty Jones waved a hand in the air.

'I figured that already, Sheriff.' The Kid smiled. 'These folks don't seem as bright as me though.'

'Where were you headed, Valko?' Scott demanded.

'Nowhere.' The outlaw sighed. 'I was looking for water for my horse and myself.'

'You were coming here to rob our bank, weren't you?' Scott blazed. 'Admit it, you bastard.'

'You ever robbed a bank?' one of the men queried.

'It says he did on the poster,' Betty Jones added.

'So you were coming here to rob our bank?' Scott exclaimed loudly.

'I don't even know where this town is, boys.' The Kid blew out long and hard at the ceiling as if trying to find some divine guidance. 'I ain't ever robbed a bank in my life.'

'But the poster quite clearly states

you have robbed banks.'

'Then the poster is wrong.' Valko smiled at the faces before him. It was a sly smile designed to make the men worry.

'I reckon he wasn't headed here, boys.' The sheriff rested a shapely hip on the edge of her desk and watched the men before her. Only the tall, slim Valko seemed to have any air of dignity about him although he was still naked from the waist up.

The men huddled again as if trying to get to grips with the problem of having such a creature within the boundaries of their town.

Then as if pulled by some invisible wire, they all turned and headed for the door in single file. All behind the striding mumbling figure of Monte Scott.

It was the sheriff who kicked the door shut behind them as she rose from the desk and headed back to the tall, handsome man in her cell. For a few seconds nothing was said between the two very different creatures.

Valko looked down on to her with eyes which now seemed clearer than when they had first encountered one another. It was as if for the first time they had truly seen each other.

'God. You are the damnedest man I've ever met.' She sighed heavily.

'How so, Sheriff?' He could sense her looking at his body with more than a little interest.

'You are a man with a story, I think.'

'You got a story or two yourself,' he smiled.

'Maybe we ought to share our stories.'

Valko nodded. He knew his exploits were recorded on the Wanted poster for anyone to read but these were not his exploits. These were the mindless violations of another who hid in his shadow. A mad man who had long haunted the name of the Valko Kid.

4

The ground was soft and damp near the waterfall which seemed to cascade from heaven itself down into the river. Clem Everett had ridden for six hours seeking a sign to point him in the correct direction and allow his posse to once again pick up Valko's trail.

He sat in his high Texan saddle watching the men filling their canteens and enjoying the cold pure mountain water without uttering a single sound. He knew this was wrong. He knew he had chosen the wrong route. Back at the creek, where they had made camp and ate heartily, the round worn pebbles offered no indication as to which way their prey had chosen to ride. It had been his call and it had led them here, but it was wrong.

The soft ground was virginal with the exception of a few animal tracks and those left by his men. There was no sign of Valko's horse ever coming anywhere near this drinking place. If he had taken this trail, he would have had to let the animal drink and that would have left tracks. He had seen the tracks of the outlaw's stallion too many times to mistake it for any other horse. The distinctive horseshoe forged back in Indian Ridge was unlike any other.

'What's eating you, Clem?' Booth Dawson drooled as he tried vainly to cope with the oversized tobacco plug in his mouth.

Everett dismounted and ventured to the river with his horse silently.

Josh Cavey filled his hat with water and placed it back on to his hot skull.

'We come the wrong way?'

'We come the wrong way, Josh.' Everett spat out the trail flies which had coated his teeth as he had ridden hard at the head of his troop of volunteers. A sickness churned his guts inside out as he tried to come to terms with the fact he had yet again made a mistake of which his prey could take full advantage.

'What?' Dawson yelled in dismay.

'I done steered us wrong, boys,' the marshal admitted.

It was a bitter pill and he disliked its flavour, but Everett was no coward and always ready to tell the truth.

'You seemed so certain . . . ' Dawson shrugged.

'We had two choices and I done steered us wrong.' The marshal's face was stiff with self-recrimination.

'We have to go all the way back?' Brad Carter, a youngster compared to the other posse members, asked.

'We do,' the marshal nodded.

'I reckon we ain't ever gonna catch that son of a . . . '

Everett looked at the sky and then back into the faces of his men. He knew how long their quest had been and the suffering it had inflicted on them all. The promise of splitting the reward money had kept this bunch together, but there were few faces left from his original posse. A man can only devote so much of his time to chasing a phantom and, unlike Everett himself, who had nothing to go home to, these men were becoming tired.

'Tomorrow is soon enough,' Everett sighed heavily.

Josh Cavey moved to the man's side.

'We gonna make camp? It's early.'

'We got time on our side and the Valko Kid's carrying one of Booth's bullets,' Everett began. 'I reckon we deserve to rest up and wash our duds. We are all stale and smell worse than our horses. Get the bed rolls off your nags and make camp, boys.'

The men did as they were instructed. None of them wanted another minute in their saddles. Not this day.

The river was cool and gently tempting. Everett knew his men would come to no harm if they obeyed his orders.

'Tomorrow we'll be fresh and our horses will be faster than Valko's,' Everett said, removing his Stetson and tossing it to the ground.

'Reckon we'll catch him tomorrow, Clem?' a voice asked.

The marshal started unbuckling his chaps. He could have answered yet he was not one to lie to his men however tempting it was to be optimistic.

5

The small office had become more a home to the old doctor than his well-furnished house two streets away. Here he had practised his trade for more years than he cared to remember but never had he felt this troubled before.

Jenks poured out a full measure of whiskey into the specimen tumbler and downed it silently. The green shades of his office window hid him from the staring eyes of passing citizens and the locked door gave the impression the office was empty. Yet the old-timer was troubled. For two hours he had sat here and brooded over something which tore at his soul.

He had once been an outlaw. He had known all the reasons which filled a man's head for riding that route but Valko seemed to be totally alien to any of these reasons.

Something just did not add up and it was eating at his well-rounded girth.

Tending the wounds of the outlaw known as the Valko Kid had made his own notorious past fill his thoughts. He knew a good man compared to a bad man when he met them and Valko was anything but the latter.

Forty years ago he had chosen the wrong trail and for a brief few months ridden hard along the outlaws' path. He had been headstrong and drank heavily then. All young men drank heavily then. That was what men did. Yet the haze of hard liquor had blurred his judgement and he had become a road agent. At first he just told himself it was simply a game, a way to outfox the stagecoach companies. Their money was his money.

Riding over 200 miles in a matter of six months, he had held up more than twenty stagecoaches and taken their strong boxes. He had spent the loot as quickly as he could so he had an excuse to go out and steal another. It had become an addiction to him. No drug could have filled his breast with the same amount of excitement. It was the ultimate thrill.

It had become so easy for the young man, he had forgotten he was stealing decent folks' life-savings. To him, he was a mythical figure like Robin Hood. He deluded himself he was not doing wrong or harm to anyone. Yet he gave nothing to the poor; he simply spent it all on orgies of fun, simply for his own pleasure and to hell with anyone else.

He was just being a young hothead letting off steam.

Jenks finished his tumbler of whiskey and shook his head as the memories came flooding back within the confines of his dark office.

Memories which chilled him to his marrow.

He had prided himself in never shooting anyone and only frightening folks into throwing down the strong boxes from the stagecoaches. One after another, he had held up the stages and taken the loot. For a while it had seemed to be the best job any fit young man could have.

Until he had targeted one stagecoach too many. It had been the midnight stage out of Deadwood. He had hidden himself twelve miles out of the violent town and waited for the sound of the six-horse team as it thundered along the narrow trail which would take it to the small town of Hangman's Bluff.

The trees were plentiful in that area and he had found no trouble in secreting himself upon his tall horse near the trail and waiting. He had an incredible patience for a man of his tender years, and found waiting half the fun. As each passing minute ticked by, his excitement grew.

Then he had heard the sound, which had become familiar to his young ears. The sound of long leather reins being whipped across the spines of the coach team.

Jenks recalled riding out from his

hiding-place and then pulling up his bandanna to cover his features. He had done the same thing so many times in so many places, it had become too easy.

He shuddered as he remembered seeing the outriders and their Winchesters gleaming in the moonlight.

Jenks poured another tall measure of the alcohol as he began to sweat. The riders had been hired to protect the stagecoach as the Overland Stage Company had begun to get a tad annoyed at the outlaw who was robbing them blind. He recalled how he had been frozen to his saddle when he had seen the riders and their long gleaming weaponry.

Before he could do anything, the outriders rained a volley of lead at him and he had somehow managed to avoid being hit by spurring his horse away.

At first it had been exciting to have so many men chasing him but as the bullets grew ever closer, he became afraid his days were numbered.

For the first time, Jenks had realized

this was no mere game he had embarked upon. This was serious and might even be fatal should he slow up his pace.

Jenks recalled riding all through the night with the men on his heels. Bullets flew over his head and past his crouched body as he urged the hapless horse on. As sunrise broke, the men were still behind him as he rode up a steep mountain trail. He had never been to this place before and nothing seemed familiar to the young eyes of the terrified outlaw. All he could do was ride and pray he might find a place where safety could protect his unworthy hide.

Jenks swallowed his whiskey as his memory burned its unrelenting messages to his old body.

Riding higher and higher through the morning dust, he had begun to notice the trees were now becoming thinner and less prominent. He was becoming an easier target for his pursuers to aim their trusty repeating rifles at. The climb was becoming harder on the tired horse, as he had forced the animal to find grip beneath its hooves where there was none. The horse tried vainly to obey its master yet the ground was not designed for such a noble animal. Even mountain goats would have had trouble keeping their feet on this slope.

Sliding backwards, the huge creature finally tumbled over and only through luck did the youthful outlaw manage to slip off the saddle and roll to a halt. Watching in horror, he saw the horse rolling down the slope before hitting a tall broad tree at the riders' feet.

Now on foot, the outlaw scrambled ever upward through the loose dust and stone. There was nowhere else to go. Only up. His hands bloodied, he clawed his way ever upward desperately. Bullets echoed as his chasers opened up on their prey. He ducked and dived as the earth around him was eaten up by the Winchester cartridges, as they exploded the ground itself into a million pieces. Then he somehow reached the summit of this dry, sun-baked mountain and for a moment thought there would be time to slide back down the other side and find refuge before they caught up with him. As the bullets tore up the ground around him he hovered in disbelief at what his eyes observed.

There was no place to roll and slide down.

He was standing on a precipice.

Before him there was only a cliff; a sheer drop into a narrow, fast-flowing river which wound its way through a billion trees. A drop of at least 200 feet.

The old doctor stood and moved to the mirror on his office wall and studied the image which reflected back at him. This was how he now looked.

Old.

Used up.

Staring through his own image his whiskey-soaked eyes closed as he remembered how he had jumped into the air off the cliff.

The fall would have killed the average man but he had been lucky and somehow survived. The water had been deep and he had been taken countless miles downstream before managing to claw his way back on to dry land.

From that moment on, Ralph Hanks the outlaw had died and a man named simply Jenks had been born. He had gone East and trained as a doctor. When he had his qualifications neatly detailed on a shingle, he returned to the West and found himself here in Bear Claw.

He could have taken it easy back East and practised on the rich folks who paid well to be told how ill they were, but he knew it was out in the West where he could do the most for his fellow man.

Jenks poured water from a jug into a bowl and splashed his face until he regained some of his composure.

The Valko Kid was said to be what he had once been, but unlike himself, Jenks felt the Kid did not fit his Wanted poster.

Jenks dried his features and unlocked

the office door and stepped out into the street. He shuddered again as he recalled the chilling lesson he had once been taught. Betty Jones had an outlaw caged in her sheriff's office but Jenks knew one thing for sure: unlike himself, Valko did not fit his reputation. Given a break, as he had once been given a break, Jenks pondered the fate of the young gunfighter.

★   ★   ★

'What you looking at, Valko?' Sheriff Betty Jones asked as her match touched the wick of the lamp upon the cluttered desk before her. She had seen the handsome features of her prisoner facing in her direction for the past hour. Even as the office became bathed in darkness she could feel the heat of his eyes as they watched her. Placing the crystal globe over the flame she adjusted the wick until the room was soaked in its strangely hypnotic warmth.

'I was thinking,' Valko responded as he sat on the edge of the cot.

'About what?'

He watched as she moved to the stove and forced a few more pieces of kindling into it.

'Is my old horse still tied up outside?'

'Sure is.' She rubbed her hands on the back of her jeans.

'Could you bring in my saddle-bags?'

She stood next to the stove and warmed her shapely backside before replying, 'What for?'

'I've got me thirty-five dollars in silver coin in them bags.'

Her face changed its expression. 'You're not figuring on trying to bribe me with thirty-five bucks, is you?'

The Kid smiled and lowered his head before standing and looking directly at her.

'Nope.'

'Then what?'

'Old Snow is not as young as he once was, ma'am.' Valko cleared his throat. 'I have ridden him hard and long for days now and he's tired. I just thought you could use the money to get him stabled in a good livery.'

Betty edged closer to the caged man. Her face softened as it sought a hint of the vicious animal described upon the Wanted poster, and found none.

'Is that all your money?' she asked.

The Kid nodded. 'Yep. That is my entire fortune.'

'And you wanna use it all to get your horse bedded up in the livery stable?'

He shrugged and reached down to the foot of the cot for his shirt.

'Are you soft, Valko?' There was a hint of teasing in her voice as her hands gripped the bars of the cell. 'Spending all your money to look after your horse?'

'He's old and he's a good horse.' Valko carefully slipped the shirt on before noticing the bullet hole and dried blood which had ruined it.

'Gimme the shirt.' Her voice was warmer than melting butter over a plate of flapjacks.

He did as instructed.

'You don't look the sort of lady who darns, ma'am,' Valko grinned as he watched her studying the shirt.

'You're right, Valko, I ain't the sort who darns,' she said moving to the stove and carefully lifting its hinged lid with the barrel of her gun.

His eyes narrowed as he watched her stuffing the shirt into the flames.

'Thanks a bundle. I ain't got another shirt and it ain't getting any warmer.'

She did not say anything. Her feet moved to the door and she stepped outside, leaving him to stand alone in the well-constructed jail. He wondered what was going on after he had waited for nearly three minutes. For the first time since becoming a caged prisoner, he truly felt the helplessness of his situation. For the first time, he began to know what it was to be captured.

Nothing happened for a further twelve minutes as Valko stood silently watching the hands of the wall clock ticking relentlessly on and on. With each movement of the minute hand as it rocked on to its next hand-painted target line, his heart seemed to pound more strongly within his naked chest. This was what it was like to be a prisoner.

As the Kid felt sweat trickling down his temple, he noticed the door opening again and the rush of relief when she re-entered the sheriff's office.

Tossing the saddle-bags on to the desk she closed the door behind her and slid the bolts.

'You were a long time,' he said rubbing the sweat off his face with a finger.

'Miss me?' Her face was rosy and her tone breathless. She had been busy. She had been rushing about, he could tell.

'Yep,' Valko heard himself saying.

She paused. Suddenly their eyes locked on to one another across the room. They said nothing as if trying to seek the truth within each other's souls.

Then he noticed the small brown paper parcel under her right arm.

'Where did you go?' he asked in a broken voice.

She walked toward him with the parcel and held it to the bars silently. Valko reached through the bars of his private prison and accepted the bundle before pulling it through the iron rods which went from floor to ceiling.

'A new shirt,' he said aloud in a surprised tone.

'A black new shirt, Valko,' Betty Jones corrected as she watched him undo the buttons.

'Why?'

'I can't have you freezing to death before I . . . ' Her voice faded away as she suddenly thought about the words which were in her mind. Words which chilled her.

'Hang me?' Valko pulled on the shirt as she watched him.

The female turned away and moved hastily to the desk where she pretended to busy herself. For some reason which she could not fathom, she was upset.

'Betty?' the Kid's voice rang across

the distance between them.

Keeping her back to him she cleared her throat before replying, 'What now, Valko?'

'You OK?' There was a genuine concern in his voice.

'Sure am.' She seemed to move about the shadows of the office without facing him for the longest time.

'If you check in the bags you'll find the money . . . ' Valko tried to see her face as he spoke, but she was determined to keep it turned away from his glare.

'I put your old horse in the livery and he's being rubbed down and pampered,' she said loudly, trying to overcome her irrational emotions.

'How much did it cost?'

'The town will cover the cost, Valko,' she blurted.

Valko gripped the bars and found himself raising his voice.

'Sheriff?'

She swung about and looked at him. Even in the shadows of the room he could see the sparkling pupils which betrayed her emotion.

'You crying for me, Betty?' Valko sighed.

For the first time in her life Betty Jones found herself unable to speak.

'Don't waste tears on me, ma'am,' Valko urged.

'Why not?' she gushed.

'I ain't worth it, Betty.'

'I'm the sheriff. I'll decide your worth, Valko.'

Valko's chin dropped on to his chest. Now the outlaw found himself unable to find the right words.

6

The sky was big and red, as red as the Devil's hide. The sun had fallen below the distant mountain range but had yet to cease its daily battle with the forces of night. Thirty miles north of Bear Claw, a lone rider mercilessly spurred his dapple-grey mount steadily towards the towering twin peaks which overlooked the mining town. He had never been here before but knew everything there was to know about the town which sat amid the millions of trees. This was a man who did his homework and left nothing to chance.

This rider wore black like the man who had been branded for all his crimes. This ruthless demon seemed to have been created in Hell itself. There were few outlaws who rode in the shadow of another, but this rider had made a fine art at doing just that.

He was a man few had ever managed to get close to without being dispatched to their Maker. Even as he rode, he kept his bandanna loose and covering his lower jaw whilst his Stetson was pulled down over his temple so his features were never seen in any great detail. He could have been of any age, for all the facial skin he displayed. Even out here in the barren wilderness where only a few homesteaders' homes dotted the scenery every dozen or so miles, he seemed concerned at never allowing anyone or anything to see his face.

These were not the actions of an eccentric but the carefully practised ploys of an outlaw who wanted folks to remember the black clothing and the horse which appeared white at a distance.

He was evil on horseback and yet as cunning as any fox in any henhouse. It had been a long while ago when he had first set eyes upon the lean youth who rode a white stallion and everyone referred to as Valko. The plan had hatched itself slowly at first in his twisted brain, but it had hatched all the same.

This man had worked out even then it would be a simple matter for him to dress as the youngster dressed, in dark clothing and make everyone believe it was the 'kid' who had murdered and robbed so ruthlessly. His pale-grey horse gave the appearance of being white in the cool dusk of night. The bandanna hid his unseen features and made it possible to fool all who witnessed his crimes. He had always been a killer and never allowed anyone or anything to stop him getting what he wanted, but disguised as the youngster known as Valko, he had thrown caution to the wind.

Now he killed for the sheer joy of knowing another innocent soul would be blamed for his actions. It had been so very simple and somehow it continued to be even simpler to perpetuate the deceit. Whenever this rider had ridden into a town and destroyed innocent people, the blame fell on to the broad shoulders of the Valko Kid.

It had made him almost forget his own identity and there was part of the cunning man who believed he truly was Valko. He had robbed a dozen banks and killed his way out of every corner he had found himself trapped in. Each bullet he fired added another nail in the coffin waiting for the real Valko Kid.

Whatever his true identity was, it remained hidden behind the bandanna which muffled his face. He knew there would come a time when the hapless Valko would finally get caught and lynched and then he would have to resort to another disguise to confuse the law. As he rode, he hoped that day was a long way off.

Even at sunset it remained hot and unforgiving as the lone rider continued heading to the place he had learned so much about, where the banks were swollen with the wealth of a gold-mining town. Dust and ore crammed into its vaults awaiting an enterprising outlaw to have the guts to take it. He knew he was such an outlaw. No other road agent would have the guts to do what he planned to do.

The rider knew he would have to plan his escape perfectly if he was going to make this job work. This job was bigger than anything he had ever tackled before. It was ambitious to say the least, but this villain had long ceased doubting his abilities. He knew this daring robbery would probably make him more than any of his previous ones. He had to work out the lay of the land before he struck. This was no town lying on the vast range where a fast horse could do all that was required. Bear Claw was high up in the pass between two mountains and had to be studied hard before he acted. This meant he had to ride into town without raising anyone's suspicions. He would have to get himself another horse on which to enter Bear Claw and entirely different clothes so he might move around without being noticed. Then and only then, when he had everything figured out perfectly, he would change into the dark clothing and use his dapple-grey horse to create the illusion the Valko Kid had struck again. It was a plan he had used several times in the past when he knew he had to be extra careful.

Bear Claw might be an apple waiting to be plucked, but this mysterious rider knew the hidden dangers all well-populated towns posed for the unwary.

He could see the glowing street lights high up in the pass as the sky finally began to darken enough for the stars to come out from their hiding places. Bear Claw was welcoming the evening, unaware of who was approaching.

Pulling hard on the reins of the grey, the man studied the small ranch below him: a ranch house sitting next to a corral filled with a dozen mounts.

Rubbing his mouth on his sleeve he laughed to himself and pulled out the

Colt from his right holster. Loading the weapon he repeated the action with his left-hand pistol. There were no notches carved upon these wooden gun grips, there had been too many victims and too little wood.

He sat silently upon the ridge soaking up the dusk as it overwhelmed him and everything about him. Only the large moon which still hung low over his shoulder gave illumination to this secluded place. He knew this was the perfect place for him to execute his plans.

Ramming his spurs into the flesh of the horse he headed down the rise toward the house. It was early evening and the coyotes were beginning to howl at the millions of twinkling stars above his head. There was an old Indian legend which said all of the creatures which roamed the Great Spirit's vast land had their likeness painted in the sky in the form of stars. All except the coyote. Which was why, every night, it howled out to the Great

Spirit begging Him to put his image in the heavens too.

The cunning outlaw gripped his reins tightly as he rode his horse down toward the ranch. He knew nothing of legends: he only knew how to steal and kill.

★　★　★

It was a well-built man who stepped out from the darkness of the ranch house carrying a seldom-used scattergun in his huge hands. Only the moon lit the bleak ranch, but both men could see all they wished to see of one another. The man by the building was rugged, the sort who carved out civilization with their bare hands and gritty determination. The rider was harder to work out: his was a face hidden behind a bandanna.

He might have been just a passing stranger wishing to water his horse but the big man had a feeling in his craw. He knew trouble when it rode in and this rider smelled of trouble.

'Hold on there, mister,' the rancher ordered.

The rider pulled up on his reins and the grey horse stopped.

'What you want?' the big man snarled trying to cover up his own fear by raising his voice.

The rider sat motionless in his saddle. The moon on his back he cast an eerie image over the homesteader.

'You gonna answer me?'

'I'm looking for something,' the rider said, in a voice which echoed around the courtyard.

'What you looking for exactly, mister?'

'Many things, old man.' The rider steadied his mount before starting to dismount. 'Money. Female company and grub.'

The triggers of the scattergun were quickly cocked and the rancher watched as the rider seated himself back in his saddle cautiously. For the briefest of moments the big man thought he had somehow won their duel of wits.

'Ain't used to being a loser, are you, mister?' the rancher gruffed.

The outlaw felt his own breath as it came back off his bandanna. His fingers were at his side as he sat astride the pale horse and watched the man before him who had probably never gunned down anything larger than a jack-rabbit.

'You seem a mite nervous,' the outlaw rasped. 'A nervous man with his fingers on the triggers of an old scattergun can be dangerous.'

'I don't cotton to folks riding in at sunset, mister.' The big man spat at the ground.

'Well I might just be here to ask if I could fill my canteen and water my grey,' the rider said through his bandanna.

'You might.'

'Or I might be here to kill you and steal a horse.' There was a sound of amusement in the riders voice. 'I might just be the fastest gunfighter you ever set eyes upon.'

The big man kept the rifle aimed up at the strange visitor.

'I don't care for your humour, mister.'

'Humour?'

'Yep. Jokes about killing ain't what I call friendly.'

The rider nodded.

'I'd agree with you if I was joking but . . . ' Faster than the confused rancher could have ever imagined, the rider had drawn and fired both his Colts. Lead lit up the evening as it ripped across the yard into the large man.

The rancher stumbled and fell on to his knees still clutching the scattergun. He was dead even before his face landed in the soft mud.

Dismounting quickly, the outlaw heard the screams coming from within the house. Two separate screaming female voices shrilled out. The door burst open allowing the lamplight to stretch across the scene.

The outlaw stood devoid of any emotion as he watched the two females rushing to the body. One woman seemed wide and was obviously the wife, whilst the second seemed slimmer and either sister or daughter to the first. Neither gave the killer a second look or thought as they rushed to the body. The howling was sickening to the man who moved closer to the females. As they knelt, trying vainly to make the big man come back to life, he holstered one of his weapons allowing himself a free hand.

'Get up,' he shouted.

It took several times for him to repeat his order before either female noticed him towering over them. He grabbed at the thinner woman first and hauled her to her feet by her hair. Then after kicking the older woman, he used the same method to drag her up out of the mud.

'Get in the house,' the outlaw snapped at them.

It required he slam them both with the barrel of his pistol before the two began to move into the dimly illuminated sod structure. Following his bleeding victims he closed the door and slid the large wooden bolt across.

'Wh . . . what are you?' the older woman screamed hysterically.

'I'm the Valko Kid,' he lied as he moved closer to them.

There was a pot hanging over a roaring fire in the grate. The smell of stew filled the crude room.

'Get me some grub, woman.' He pointed at the younger female who was attractive apart from the mark across her cheek where his gun had whipped her.

'Why did you kill my Rufus?' the older woman yelled as she wrung her fingers together trying to milk the air itself.

'Shut up or I'll kill you next,' he snarled.

The younger woman ladled stew on to a tin plate and placed it upon the large wooden table.

Dragging a chair across the room, the outlaw sat training his weapon on the two terrified females whilst he used a spoon to gather up the thick stew.

'Why did you kill my pa?' the younger woman cried as she hugged her sobbing mother. 'My pa was a good man.'

'Now he's just a dead sodbuster.' The outlaw chewed the food as he toyed with his gun. 'Nobody will ever give a damn about the loss of a sodbuster.'

'He was my husband, you evil — '

'This your daughter?' the chewing killer asked as his attention fell upon the younger woman briefly.

'She is.'

'She looks big and healthy.' The man grinned. 'I like big healthy women.'

'You gonna take our horses?' the younger female asked.

'I require a place to hole up in.' The man nodded. 'I'll take one of your horses but that will be afterwards.'

'After what?' the younger woman asked fearfully.

'After I've taken you and her.' The outlaw chewed relentlessly until his plate had been cleared of food then he rose to his feet and stepped closer to the two shaking creatures before him.

The mother moved angrily at him as if filled with an emotion she had never before discovered within herself. Her broken nails tried to rip at his flesh. He smashed the gun across her head and stepped astride as she fell at his feet. The daughter stared in disbelief at her mother as if unable to move. Stepping over the downed woman, the man closed in on her as she tried to back away in a room which had no hiding places.

His free hand grabbed her collar and ripped the fragile material down to her waist. It tore easily in his strong grip and he pulled her closer. His savage eyes focused upon her firm supple breasts as they bore witness to her immaturity. She had never even been courted before and out here in the wilderness of a new land seldom saw any men apart from the man who lay out in the mud. To her this was nothing more than a nightmare which she felt sure she would awaken from soon.

To him, this female was just something to use, something to violate; a mere object to satisfy his loins. Unlike his usual conquests, she would not cost him any money. This one would be free and might just be all the sweeter for that simple fact.

She felt the whiskers rubbing over her face and then down her body. There seemed to be nothing she could or should do. She, like all females of her kind, had never been told anything about men and what they did. To her, this might be the way it was supposed to be. As he dragged her into the room where her bed waited, she felt numb.

Even when he threw her on to the top of the bed and began tearing at her undergarments she just lay there staring at the ceiling which seemed to move in the flickering of the light from the fire-place in the main room.

As the man holstered his gun he unbuckled the gun-belt and laid it down on the floor before fumbling with his trousers. She watched as he crawled up between her legs and began to cry. Then she felt his hot flesh forcing itself within her body. A pain ripped through her innocence.

A wiser soul would have known this was wrong, but she had no knowledge of wisdom. All she knew was this was no dream she would soon awaken from, but a living nightmare.

7

Valko ran the crust of bread around the rim of his plate before consuming the last of his supper. Blowing out hard, the outlaw bent down from the edge of the cot and rested the plate on the floor next to the empty coffee mug. It had been his first square meal in over two weeks. He studied the female who was still eating at the desk silently. She was one gritty woman and if he was any judge, only in her early to mid-twenties. How she had been elected to the position of sheriff over a townful of men seemed too strange to even try and figure out. Yet the Valko Kid had never shunned the tough questions.

'How come they voted you in as sheriff, ma'am?' he found himself asking as she stood wiping her mouth on a crisp blue napkin.

'Bear Claw is full of smart folks,

Valko.' Betty Jones grinned and ambled toward the coffee pot perched upon the stove top.

'Must be.'

Pouring herself another cup of the strong black liquid she cast her sights on him.

'I can't figure you,' she admitted.

'Mine is a long story, ma'am.' Valko ran his fingers through his thick black hair and tried to ignore her tempting form as it hovered next to the hot black stove.

'Another cup of java?' She raised the pot and strode toward his cell.

He stared at the silver-tipped boots she sported and then allowed himself to take in her full form. Although dressed in shirt and jeans, she was a sight which made even the weary outlaw take notice. Picking up the mug he stood and pushed it through the bars before watching her fill it.

'I like long stories, Valko,' Betty Jones said in a soft tone unlike any which he had heard come from the well-shaped lips previously. 'I think we ought to talk.'

'I ain't the varmint described on the Wanted poster.' Valko blew at the rising steam which circled the rim of his mug.

She rested her bottom on a hard chair beside the cell and placed the coffee pot between them on the floor.

'You telling me you ain't the Valko Kid?' There was a look of puzzlement in the beautiful face.

'Nope. I'm called Valko, but there's another critter out there someplace who has robbed trains and the like. Killed a lot of innocent folks and worse. He wears black and rides a horse similar to my Snow. Reckon it serves his purpose to let folks think he's me.'

'That's a real tall story.' She sipped at her steaming beverage and watched the man closely. However hard she stared she could see no hint of this man lying.

'Tall but true.' The Kid sat on the edge of his cot and swallowed the black brew thoughtfully.

'Why would anyone do such a thing?'

Betty found herself being drawn to the man whom she had caged.

'Maybe he's just loco. Maybe he's cunning. Who can figure?'

There was a sound in the outlaw's voice which had an emptiness about it. It was as if he no longer felt he would ever find peace and doubted his sanity for even trying to clear his name.

'You telling me the truth?' Betty Jones stared straight at his face. There was nowhere to hide. He had to look straight back at her and for the second time it was if they could read each other's deepest thoughts.

'I've been known to brag, but lying ain't my style,' he confessed. 'My ma once told me a liar has to have a good memory and to tell the truth I ain't ever had much of a memory. I've always found being honest a tad easier.'

'When I caught you why did you tell me your name?' Betty Jones rested her coffee mug on to the floor and stood. 'If you had lied to me I might never have figured out who you were.'

'Maybe I'm not very smart, ma'am.' Valko gave a long sigh.

'Reckon it could be you just ain't dishonest, Valko.' Her frown softened to a smile. 'I must be going loco but I believe you.'

The Valko Kid rose to his feet and gripped the iron bars in his hands. She believed in him. It seemed impossible but she actually believed in him. For a man who rode trying to avoid the deadly bullets of people intent on killing him for the reward money, being believed made him seem to grow even taller than he already was.

Betty moved closer to the cell until her body was pressing against his. Only the metal rods were between them as she heaved her ample bosom excitedly. He could feel her heart pounding almost as quickly as his own, but was troubled.

'You ain't no outlaw, Valko,' Betty purred, like a kitten facing a bowl of fresh cream. 'I've seen a lot of saddle tramps in my time but you have an honesty about you. No ruthless killer would have turned down the chance of grabbing my six-gun.'

He soaked in her scent. It soothed his tortured soul but he still pulled away from her and moved to the far wall of the small cell. Resting his brow on his forearm he blew heavily at the floor. She wanted him and he sure liked her, but he knew this could bring her nothing but trouble and heartache. The Valko Kid had never taken advantage of anyone and he sure wasn't starting now, even if it meant remaining caged like the animal he was claimed to be.

'Don't I interest you, Valko?' Her eyes seemed bigger as she stared across the cell to where he stood brooding.

'Oh, you interest me, Sheriff,' the Kid admitted. 'I can sure testify to that. You interest me a whole lot.'

'Then what's the matter?' Betty was confused by the look of sadness which etched his handsome features.

Raising his head to face her Valko pointed his thumbs at his chest and gritted his teeth.

'Look at me, Betty. I'm the Valko Kid. Wanted either dead or possibly alive. I'm worth twenty-five thousand dollars either way.' His head dropped and his chin touched his chest. 'You're a good kid and you believe me, which makes me proud, but I'm still wanted. Think about it.'

There was a silence in Betty Jones as she moved across to her desk and picked up the large key ring and then returned. In amazement, he watched as she pushed the key into the cell door lock and twisted it. The sound of the bolt being released shocked him as he rubbed his neck watching her swinging the door open.

'I don't get it, Betty.' Valko could not believe his eyes as he studied her approaching.

Walking into the cell she cornered the tall man. She reached up and pulled his head down until she found his lips with hers. There had been few men who had ever managed to get this close to the attractive sheriff of Bear Claw before and Valko sensed this. As he dragged her willing body off the floor in his strong arms he recalled the last town where he had found a brief moment of happiness with someone equally as beautiful yet very different to this wondrous creature.

Nestling his face into her soft hair he felt her lips tracing patterns along his unshaven face. He felt as if he were betraying the girl he had left behind in Indian Ridge, but without Betty all he faced was a hangman's noose.

Life was too short for him to deny himself one last moment of humanity. After all, how far behind him was the relentless posse which never gave up its pursuit?

Valko knew it was wrong, but so was dying for another man's crimes.

'Now do you get it?' Betty purred again.

'I get it, ma'am.'

8

The stranger who rode into Bear Claw wore a large buckskin jacket with its collar turned up. It had belonged to the dead rancher he had so ruthlessly gunned down and left bleeding in the ranch yard thirty miles south. The rancher no longer required it nor his two females either. The outlaw had used them too. No longer astride his pale dapple-grey horse he had saddled one of the sorrels from back on the ranch, to where he would return to the two women he had left bound and gagged. Then he would once again dress in black and ride the grey and become Valko, so his latest crimes would be added to the long list.

The town was quieter than he had expected for a gathering place for gold miners, yet he was not concerned. He was here for only one purpose and that was to get the lay of the land before he struck.

This rider kept his hat pulled down over his hair so he could see and not be recognized. This was the man the Valko Kid had sought for so long. As the rider spurred the sorrel past the quiet sheriff's office he had no idea how close he was to the man who had been branded by his savage actions. No idea how close the real Valko Kid was.

Passing saloon after saloon, he studied the streets and every alley which might prove valuable. The streets were illuminated by dozens of coal-oil lamps whose light seemed to mix with the strange glowing moon above his head. There was a haze about the light which troubled the rider. One street after another the man steered the horse as he attempted to memorize the entire layout of Bear Claw.

Not once nor even twice, but three times he travelled every single street within the town's ramshackle boundaries. On the third passing he pulled the horse to a halt and studied the huge building.

The bank was built to last from imported brick and stone. The rider sat motionless opposite the town square taking in every detail of the solid structure. It bore little resemblance to any bank he had ever encountered before. This building could have graced the streets of any large Eastern city. It would have seemed out of place in Bear Claw had it not been for the town's reputation of having a fortune in gold crammed within its vault. Gold had built not only the town but this massive dwelling place for the valuable ore. For a moment the rider seemed disheartened as he pondered the three-storey structure.

Robbing it might prove impossible for one gun, he thought.

The rider placed a cigar between his cracked lips and struck a match across the saddle horn. Inhaling the smoke he thought about the situation.

It was a problem he had not

anticipated but he had never shied away from mere problems. His was the mentality of the man who knew how to turn a problem into a challenge.

To get gold out of Bear Claw's bank would prove to be almost impossible unless the job was tackled from a different angle and this man knew every angle there was.

Allowing the smoke to linger within his lungs, the evil man knew the easiest way to get something out of a place such as this was to force others to do it for him. Humans were weak, whilst the walls of this bank were strong and impenetrable. Most bankers were the weakest sort of human life, thought the outlaw as he sucked the acrid smoke even deeper into his lungs before allowing it to filter back out of his mouth slowly.

The weakest link had to be anyone with a set of keys and a loved one they would hate to see tortured for a saddle-bag full of golden dust or nuggets. All he had to do was locate the critter who would steal the riches for him, given the right incentive.

Spurring the drab horse down the long street, he closed in on what appeared to be the richest of all the saloons he had observed as he had ridden around Bear Claw.

Dismounting the nervous animal, he tossed the reins over the hitching rail and secured the leather laces tightly. This was not an animal he trusted to stay where it was left. Stepping up on to the boardwalk, the man confidently entered the noisy building.

The smoke, noise and smell hit him hard as he moved into the brilliantly lit drinking palace. Never had the outlaw seen such splendour draped upon walls. This place oozed with class and he knew men of wealth must frequent here regularly just to pay its overheads. The outlaw walked steadily towards the distant bar amid hundreds of heaving bodies. Females clad in feathers and a little lace ran from one corner to another followed by men who seemed far too old and rich to be chasing them, but they were chasing them all the same. Casting an eye upward, the man observed the dozens of doors where the girls took their eager customers.

This was a place at which civilization had yet to wag a disapproving finger. Here, men of all classes wallowed in their own excesses much as he had always done. It seemed strange to see such well-dressed men rubbing shoulders with common miners, but here only money or the lack of it, created obstructions.

Miners clad in the grime of hard graft seemed content to play cards and dice whilst rubbing shoulders with well-dressed men who were either gentlemen, pimps or cardsharps. The outlaw could not distinguish any obvious difference.

The man who had lived in the shadow of the Valko Kid managed to weave his way through the crowd successfully and finally rested his elbows on to the gleaming thirty-foot-long polished mahogany bar top.

This was no place for a man to get drunk. Not a man such as himself. He drank slowly and watched and listened. His ears were tuned to hear words which would be of use to him.

After ten minutes he heard the words he had sought.

'Mister Mayor,' one man said, next to the outlaw's elbow.

'How are you, Brooks?' came the returning volley of words.

The outlaw nodded to himself as he watched the two men in the long mirror which hung over the back wall of the bar. Carefully he absorbed the features of these two men. He had noted the name on the brass plate outside the bank that read HORACE BROOKS, PRESIDENT, BANK OF BEAR CLAW.

Turning to one of the half-sober men beside him, the narrow-eyed outlaw leaned down.

'That the banker?' he asked.

'Sure is, the tight-arsed bastard,'

came the truthful response.

The outlaw began to drift away from the bar still holding his glass of whiskey as he tracked the two large well-fed men around the massive saloon. He never got close enough to be noticed and was never far enough away from the pair to lose contact with their conversation.

Most of the words which were exchanged between Monte Scott and the banker were of such length, the outlaw could not understand them. Yet there were notable exceptions, mainly concerning gold.

After another fifteen minutes of following the two men, the fatter of the pair broke off and headed for the door. The outlaw ambled casually behind the banker at a safe distance.

Horace Brooks had no idea he was being followed as he waddled back along the dark, dimly lit streets towards his more than generous home.

The outlaw watched as Brooks entered the building which, like the bank, was made to last. Turning on his heels, the man returned to the saloon and soon located the other figure he now knew was the mayor.

Walking casually up to Monte Scott, who was observing a poker game, the outlaw deliberately bumped into the man, causing the mayor to spill his glass of whiskey.

'Gee, I'm sorry, mister.' The outlaw touched the brim of the borrowed Stetson.

'No problem, friend,' the mayor shrugged.

'Let me buy you a refill.'

'There's no need,' Scott smiled.

'I insist.' The outlaw led the overweight politician back to the long bar and bought two more whiskies.

Scott seemed to have drunk far more than his limit and was almost ready to fall down.

'Do I know you, stranger?'

'Sure. We met last spring,' the outlaw lied, keeping his hat brim pulled down over his face.

'Of course. I remember,' Scott blurted.

'I'm a friend of old Horace Brooks.'

'You just missed him.' Scott pointed feebly at the door. 'He had to go home to the little lady.'

'Does old Horace have any kids?' The outlaw struck a match and lit his cigar again.

'No. Horace never fathered anything except a lot of money.' The Mayor laughed aloud trying to steady himself.

The outlaw looked up at the bartender and placed a couple of silver dollars before him.

'Bring the mayor another couple of whiskies, barkeep,' he said.

'Why, thank you, stranger.' The council leader blinked slowly before realizing his companion had gone as quickly as he had appeared.

'You know that critter, Mister Mayor?' the bartender asked as he pulled the cork from a bottle.

'Sure. I've known him for years. Salt of the earth.'

The outlaw gathered up his reins outside the saloon and stepped into his stirrup. He had learned all he had to learn and was returning to the ranch and the two females. Tomorrow night he would return as the Valko Kid.

9

Doc Jenks turned towards the street lamp and held his gold hunter watch beneath its orange glow. It was ten after nine and the whiskey he had consumed earlier finally had worn off. Placing the watch carefully into his vest pocket, the old man faced the sheriff's office door again and knocked, once more.

The shade was moved slightly ajar and the medical man caught just a brief glimpse of the attractive female's face before he heard the bolt being reluctantly slid across. She opened it and allowed the gentle old man to enter before closing it behind him and relocking it.

'Betty,' Jenks said, removing his hat as he stepped inside the dimly illuminated office. She walked coyly past him before clearing her throat.

'Jenks,' Betty Jones said moving to

her chair behind the desk as the old-timer stood in the centre of the room.

His were wise eyes which never missed anything however trivial. He could see she was embarrassed and also Valko was sitting in a cell with the door wide open. Something had occurred since he had last been in this solid structure which he had not expected to occur. Something he thought neither of them had imagined possible a few hours prior.

'How come you ain't in bed sleeping, Jenks?' her voice asked as she seated herself behind the desk.

Jenks cast a smiling face in her direction.

'It's been a long while since I seen Betty Jones blushing.'

The sheriff tried to find a place where she might hide her face from the soft wrinkled eyes of the old doctor, but there was nowhere safe from his knowing glance.

'Jenks?' she blurted.

The old man edged towards her and rested the palms of both hands upon the wide cluttered desk.

'Is he as bad as the poster reckons, Betty?'

'Jenks, quit your teasing.' Valko's voice was as strong as he himself had always been.

Jenks looked at the man over his shoulder who stood within the confines of a cell whose door was wide open.

'How is it you ain't walked out of that cell, Valko?' Jenks asked. 'It seems to me, a crazed outlaw like the Valko Kid would not stay inside a jail when the door is open. So how come you are still in there?'

Valko's face went a sudden shade of pink as he looked at the face of the female sitting behind the desk and then at the old doctor.

'I guess I don't have an answer for you, Jenks,' he drawled sheepishly.

'I do.' Jenks moved across the room and did not stop until he was standing beside the open door of the cell.

'Let me hear it,' Valko sighed.

'Whoever's description is on the poster, it ain't yours.' Jenks eyeballed the younger man knowingly.

The Kid blew out hard as he felt another sudden rush of faith in him being freely given.

'It ain't, Jenks. You're right.'

'I figured.' Jenks pulled a hard chair towards him and sat down watching the tall man tucking his shirt back into his pants.

'I'm the victim of mistaken identity.'

'You mean that you ain't really the Valko Kid?' Jenks rubbed his chin thoughtfully as he toyed with his hat.

'Oh I'm Valko all right.' The Kid moved to the open cage door and gripped the cold iron frame in his hand. 'Leastways, I've always been tagged with the nickname of Valko since I was a young brat.'

'I don't get it.' Jenks looked at the man with eyes which had seen more than he cared to recall in his long lifetime. 'If you are Valko . . . '

'A long time ago I was in a town,' Valko began explaining. 'I remember another man there at the same time. He rode a horse something like mine. He also wore dark clothing like me.'

'Who was this man?' Jenks moved to the edge of his seat.

Valko shrugged. 'I never found out the man's name. All I know is he was a killer and he set about murdering and robbing in the town. First thing I knew, the folks there blamed me. I was flung in a jail and waiting to be hanged.'

'This other man?'

'He rode off leaving me to take the blame,' Valko snarled at the ground as he thought about the man.

'Did he look like you?' Jenks asked.

'Nope. It didn't matter none though. He wore a bandanna to cover his face and made every damn effort to tell the few witnesses who survived it was Valko who robbed the bank and killed so eagerly.'

'How did you get out of jail?'

'I had a friend who broke me out, but

he was killed.' Valko kicked his boot at the dusty floor. 'I got blamed for that too.'

'And since then you've been on the run?' Jenks stood and closed the distance between himself and the solid younger man.

Valko looked at the face of the doctor. It was a good face.

'Ever since,' he muttered.

'How have you made a living?'

'I've usually worked as a ranch hand whenever I've managed to slip the posse for a while,' Valko replied.

'Would you recognize the man who pretends to be you if you ever saw him again, Valko?' Betty Jones's voice cut through the air as she moved to the stove and fed it more kindling.

'I would. His face is carved into my memory,' Valko growled.

It was a warm hand which rested briefly on the outlaw's shoulder. Jenks knew he had been correct when he first set eyes upon him.

'I reckon we are in a slight stew,' the

doctor said looking at Betty's troubled face.

'How come?' Valko looked down at Jenks curiously.

'I don't think Betty here wants to hand you over to a lynch mob, Valko.' Jenks moved to the stove with his hands outheld trying to find warmth from its cast-iron frame as the flames licked up from its vents.

Betty Jones's face went pale as if every ounce of blood had suddenly been drained from its beautiful profile. She looked at the two men before concentrating on the elderly doctor.

'Lynch mob?' she stammered.

'Yep, Betty. That's what this young fella is looking at. A lynch mob who'll string him up. Get the town photographer to take a few shots of the body outside the funeral parlour before claiming the reward money.' Jenks rubbed his hands together over the stove as his chilling words found their target. 'You don't think Valko is gonna be allowed to live a second longer than

115

necessary, do you?'

'What about the trial?' Betty grabbed the old man's sleeve as she shook with the horror of the situation.

Jenks chuckled drily. 'What trial, Betty? The Valko Kid is wanted dead or alive. There don't have to be any trial for the likes of his sort. The decision has been already made. Dead or alive means dead, girl.'

She seemed to pace about the office as if not knowing where to head. Finally it was the strong hands of Valko which stopped her in her tracks. He held her firmly until she cast her large eyes up at him. They searched each other's souls for answers.

There were none.

Jenks moved to the pair who just focused on one another and placed a hand on each of them.

'We gotta have a plan, children.'

'Plan?' Valko stared at Jenks.

The old man nodded. 'We have to devise a plan which will allow you to get out of Bear Claw without anyone knowing what has occurred. You ain't mended yet, but I figure you ought to ride out tonight if you can, otherwise Scott and his cronies will start building a gallows out there in the town square.'

'Tonight?' Betty gasped, as the truth in the old man's words sank in.

'A moment longer and it'll be touch and go, Betty.' Jenks rested a hand on her shaking arm.

'You want to be part of a jail-break, Jenks?' The Kid followed the two people to the table where a few chairs awaited them. All three sat down and faced each other across the polished wooden surface of the varnished pine.

'I'm not what everybody thinks I am either, Valko,' Jenks imparted.

'Jenks?' Betty's eyes were moist with the thoughts he had implanted into her brain.

The man known as Jenks began to tell them his story, the story of an outlaw who luckily found salvation and became the man before them. It was a story neither she nor Valko found easy to believe but believe it they did. If there was one thing Jenks was, he was a man nobody ever could accuse of lying.

10

It was midnight when the door of the sheriff's office opened and the two figures ventured out into the misty street. The glowing lamps flickered as the wind whistled through their glass frames atop the poles which were dotted at fifty-foot intervals along the quiet thoroughfare. For a moment they both paused as the smaller Betty Jones weighed up the situation before them.

'Stick to me like glue, Kid,' she ordered the tall outlaw.

The Valko Kid moved behind the silent female along the boardwalks. He carried his saddle-bags over his shoulder and wore the pair of matched Colts in their fancy holsters on the hand-tooled belt strapped around his hips. His Stetson was pulled down over his temple so only his flashing eyes could be seen as he trailed the slim woman.

Eyes which were racked with pain as he moved. His wound had begun to burn with the effort of carrying the weight of the bags and the deadly gunbelt. What he needed was sleep, not this enforced attempt to escape.

Yet he said nothing. Where she led, he followed.

They were headed for the livery stable.

As they turned a corner, the town suddenly appeared to come to life. Here the first of dozens of saloons were still plying their trade to all who had the money to waste. There seemed to be no shortage of customers if the noise was anything to go by. Tinny pianos and various levels of voices swam out from every other doorway.

The light and sound of each of these drinking parlours seemed to merge into one frenzied soup of drunken enjoyment. Valko pulled the sheriff back as a dozen or more men staggered out into the street before them and somehow managed to walk across the wide distance to another saloon.

Betty Jones turned and looked up into the face of the man behind her which showed the strain of recent events.

'You OK, Valko?' she whispered as yet another group of men passed close by them making their way from one saloon to another.

Sweat beads sparkled on his face as he tried to smile.

'I'm fine, Betty,' he lied.

Once again she led the way. This time she moved off the boardwalk and walked behind a dozen horses which were tied up along the street. The outlaw somehow kept pace with her as she wove a path in and out of every available shadow. With every step, the Valko Kid felt his strength seeping from him the way his blood had done a couple of days back. He was weak and yet did not want her to know it. She was upset enough without her knowing the truth about his condition.

Finally they were at the livery stable

where a single lantern illuminated the interior. Betty Jones slipped through the open doorway and walked inside the structure. Turning to her left she paced to where a small tack-room stood in the blackness. Valko staggered into the darkness and gazed around the numerous stalls until he spotted the white stallion. The horse snorted in recognition of its master but the Kid was too feeble to take another step.

'Freddie?' she shouted.

The sound of a man waking up was unmistakable as a bald man struck a match and put the flame to a candle.

Valko leaned against the wooden wall and watched as the figure blinked and rubbed his tired eyes.

'Sheriff?' the sleepy voice croaked.

'Yep, it's me, Freddie. Get your butt out here.'

'Wait till I gets my britches on, ma'am,' the voice struggled.

Betty Jones moved back to Valko and ran a hand over his damp face. He was burning up.

'You don't look so good, Kid,' she muttered.

'I don't feel too good,' Valko admitted.

'This ain't gonna work.'

'It has to work, Betty.' Valko attempted to move away from the wall but felt his head filling with the haze which had dogged him upon their first meeting. It seemed so long ago to the tall outlaw. So very long ago.

'You can't ride like this, Valko.' Betty took the bags off his shoulder and dropped them to the floor as she held the man up against the wall.

The bald livery man walked out of the tack-room and up to the pair.

'What's wrong with this man, Sheriff?'

'Drunk, Freddie,' Betty said. 'You know how these saddle bums are when they hit town.'

'He don't smell drunk, ma'am,' Freddie said slowly.

'I reckon we ought to take him to my office.' She indicated with a flick of her head for the bald man to assist her. 'Give me a hand, Freddie.'

'He'll be better when he's slept it off, Sheriff.' Picking the saddle-bags up off the ground, Freddie took most of Valko's weight and did as he was instructed.

The Valko Kid said nothing as he was taken back to the sheriff's office. His was a mind filled with the mist of pain as it swirled within his skull.

As Jenks stared at Valko, as he slept on the cot in the cell he turned to the sheriff who was bolting the door after the livery man had left the office.

'Valko needs time, Betty. Time to regain his strength fully.'

'Time is something we might be a bit shy of, Jenks.'

11

Valko awoke suddenly as if his dreams had been filled with all the horrors this side of Hell. For a moment he failed to recognize either of the two people sitting at the nearby table who had tended him through the long hours of darkness as he had wrestled with the fever which had burned relentlessly, soaking his clothing and the rough blanket which covered him.

Jumping to his feet, the outlaw stared around the office and only relaxed when he noticed the cell door was wide open. Then he felt a rush of relief pouring over him as he saw the two people moving in his direction.

Jenks placed a hand on the brow of the young man, and then smiled broadly.

'The fever's broke,' he said, happily.

'How do you feel now, Valko?' Betty

asked, as she moved close to the man she had found herself unable to ignore.

Valko shook his head. 'What happened? How did I get back here?'

'You fainted again,' Betty grinned.

'I ain't never fainted in my life,' Valko protested.

'You passed out, Kid,' Jenks said, as he continued to give the standing man an examination.

'See. I didn't faint at all, I passed out,' Valko sighed.

'Men don't faint,' Betty nodded, and continued to smile as she moved out of the cell and toward the wall clock. It was nearly seven and the sun was already high enough to have filled the streets of Bear Claw with its warming rays.

Valko followed the beautiful female with the doctor at his side. As he drew close to the shapely sheriff, he could sense she was troubled.

'What's wrong, Betty?' he asked.

Jenks raised the shade to the window

126

on the side of the office which faced into a lane.

'It's a new day, Kid.'

'I messed up,' Valko said angrily, as he began to understand why she was looking so concerned.

Betty turned to the two men, her face drawn and pale.

'What are we gonna do? Darkness would have allowed Valko to ride out of here unnoticed but now it would be almost impossible.'

'We had better try and bluff our way through another day,' Jenks responded.

'Then tonight you can ride out of here, Valko.' Betty began to smile again, but this time it was Valko's face which seemed troubled. 'What's wrong, Valko?'

'The posse.'

'What posse?' Jenks mused.

'The posse which has been dogging my trail for days and shot me.' Valko moved to the coffee pot and felt it with the back of his hand.

'How close were they?'

'Close enough to be riding into Bear Claw at any moment.' The outlaw gave a sigh and rubbed his unshaven chin.

'That puts a whole new light on our problem.' Jenks began to pace about the office as he tried to once again formulate a plan.

Betty wrapped herself around the outlaw. She fitted like a glove, but the Kid just stood and watched the old man over her head. He knew the next twelve hours might bring more than a bunch of angry riders into Bear Claw. Trouble had never been far behind him.

Jenks nodded knowingly at the tall outlaw. The elderly man was still desperately trying to think of a solution which might allow the Valko Kid to survive at least one more day.

12

Monte Scott marched down the long street with his fellow council members at his heels. They had made a decision. It was brutal and yet to them totally proper. Now they were to tell the sheriff and expected no arguments or even the slightest problem.

When Valko heard the sound of a fist hitting the door of the office he glanced at Jenks and then Betty. For a few seconds his heart stopped beating.

Jenks moved to his side and hustled the tall man back into the cell. Valko was still wearing his gunbelt as he felt the healing hands forcing him down on to the bunk and covering him with the rough blanket.

'Lie there, and whatever happens don't move,' Jenks ordered.

'But . . . ' the outlaw began to speak as he felt his head being rammed down on to the cot.

'Shut up, Kid. Pretend to be unconscious.'

Jenks closed the cell door and turned the key in the lock before extracting it and tossing it on to the desk where Betty Jones was standing.

Scott's fist began hammering again as the outraged mayor shouted.

Jenks moved close to the female.

'Valko is near death's door. That's our story. That's why I'm here, Betty.'

She nodded and rubbed the tears from her cheeks as she moved to the door. Sliding the bolt across she opened the door and watched as the troop of men charged in arrogantly.

Monte Scott moved up to the cell bars and stared in at the motionless figure of the outlaw hidden beneath the blanket.

'Wake him up, Sheriff,' Scott demanded.

Jenks coughed and waited until all their eyes were upon him before he spoke.

'Valko is in a bad way, Monte.'

The mayor stepped closer to the old man.

'What do you mean?'

'I figure he might be dying,' Jenks lied, as he walked around them trying to think on his feet. 'He took a turn for the worse last night and collapsed.'

'He looked OK yesterday, Jenks.' Scott narrowed his eyes and squinted down at the still body on the cot.

'I know. The trouble started late. He began to burn up with a fever and I had to give him a sleeping draught.' Jenks ran his hands together as he felt the hot breath of the men on his neck as he paced.

'How could he be dying?' one of Scott's men queried.

'Lead poisoning,' Jenks heard himself saying as the men surrounded him.

Scott seemed confused as he looked up at the stony face of Betty Jones. She tried to appear indifferent, but it took every ounce of her strength to maintain the illusion.

'We have decided to hang him as soon as possible, Sheriff.'

Her features did not change, as she seated herself behind the desk and began fumbling with papers.

'Who decided?'

'The town council, Sheriff.' Scott added, 'We took a vote at an emergency meeting last night.'

'Makes sense,' she nodded as the men moved about her office behind the restless mayor. 'I sure hope he don't die before you can build the gallows.'

Scott glared down at her before opening the door allowing the sound of hammering to fill the office.

'Hear that?'

'What is it?' Betty asked.

'Five of my men busy in the town square building a gallows.'

She stood and moved towards Jenks. She suddenly realized he had been correct in his theory as to what Scott and his cronies would do to Valko.

'When will it be completed?' she asked in a low voice designed to sound unconcerned.

'Tomorrow it will be ready.' Scott seemed full of excitement as he nodded to every sound of hammering echoing around them. 'Tomorrow we will test the trap and then hang the bastard.'

'Why the rush, Monte?' Jenks asked seriously.

The hard-nosed mayor was not used to anyone questioning his or his committee's decisions. Yet old Jenks was a different kettle of fish. This was a man who had never shied away from asking difficult questions.

'Then we can claim the reward money,' Scott sneered.

Jenks nodded sadly. 'The town sure could use twenty-five thousand dollars.'

'Don't get smart, old man,' Scott raged, as he grabbed the handle and thrust open the door and marched out on to the boardwalk. 'You just get him fit enough so we can hang him.'

A chill overcame the doctor as he

watched the attractive female closing the door after the last of the men departed the office.

'You were dead right, Jenks,' Betty Jones mumbled, as she slid the bolt across the door. 'They would hang Valko even if he was already dead.'

Jenks said nothing. Whenever he dwelt upon his fellow man's inhumanity it upset him.

* * *

The group of riders who rode into Bear Claw as the town clock struck eleven took all by surprise. These were not the usual drifters who visited the small settlement as they were passing through the twin mountain peaks. These were men who had long been on the trail and it showed.

United States Marshal Clem Everett led the riders with a silence which was awesome. His features did not betray him as he glared ahead. He had watched in satisfaction as the people scattered before his posse. People had never seen such a band before riding through their town. These were men on a mission.

They were not intent upon spreading the gospel, theirs was a mission to find the man who had long eluded them. Only the Valko Kid, dead, would satisfy them.

Everett had spotted the small hand-painted sign outside the sheriff's office and was guiding his riders toward it. They followed holding an array of different rifles in their solid wind-burned hands. Resting the rifle stocks against their saddle horns, they closed in on the small insignificant office. One by one the riders drew level with their leader as he stepped from his saddle and tossed the reins over his horse's lathered neck and wrapped them around the hitching rail.

One by one his men followed suit and dismounted.

The marshal stared at the drawn

shutters with curiosity as he took the two steps toward the door. Twisting its handle he seemed surprised by it being locked.

'Can I help you folks?' The feminine voice from behind them caused each of the bedraggled posse to turn. Betty Jones paid their trail-weary comments no mind as she strode through their ranks up on to the wooden walkway beside Everett.

'A woman sheriff?' Everett exclaimed.

'I'm twice the shot any of you are, Marshal.' She pushed her key into the lock and turned it forcefully.

Everett moved towards her, but felt the strong small hand as it hit his vest buttons.

'You stopping me entering your damn office, honey?' the marshal asked in his most cold voice.

'First you tell me what you're doing in my town.' Her voice matched his for sheer volume.

Everett heard the laughter of his men as they stood beside their mounts.

'I'm leading this posse and I'm tired, missy.'

'There's a hotel just a few hundred feet down the street,' she snapped.

'We are hunting a bastard known as the Valko Kid.' Everett sighed heavily as he leant against the door frame.

'I'm afraid you and your boys are a little late.' She pushed the door open and indicated to the cell and the cot within.

Everett growled as his eyes focused on the blanket.

'You telling me you have Valko in your jail?'

'Yep. I caught him myself, Marshal.' Her words chilled them.

Everett pushed past her and moved to the bars. He stared down at the motionless bundle and cursed.

'Get up, Kid. Get up and face me.'

Betty Jones ambled to the man's side before staring up into his filthy trail-worn features.

'He can't hear you.'

'He ain't dead?' Everett gasped down at her.

'Nearly but not quite.' She moved around the man and studied him closely. He looked the way all bounty-hunters looked.

'Explain.'

'He was wounded and took a turn for the worse.'

'I want him, missy.' Everett grabbed the cell bars and tried vainly to rip them from their foundations. 'He's mine.'

'Not hardly, Marshal.' She moved to the stove and poured herself a coffee as the growling man moved behind her snorting his venom into her long loose hair. 'Finders keepers.'

'You stupid little bitch.' Everett grabbed her shoulder and pulled her around. 'Unlock the cell and let my boys take him.'

'You touch me again and I'll kill you.'

Slowly, Clem Everett began to believe her. There was no mistaking the fire in her eyes nor the magnitude of her faith in her own ability. She meant what she said.

'You sure are spunky for a female, Sheriff.'

'I'm willing to back up my words with lead, Marshal. The question is: are you?' Betty Jones watched as the man backed away from her and stared down at the cot within the cell.

'What's wrong with him?' he asked.

'Lead poisoning.'

'Our lead.' Everett spat at the floor. 'We shot him a few days back.'

'Back shooters.' She sipped her coffee.

'He was running away.'

'I still don't cotton to back shooters.' Betty rested the palm of her hand on the grip of her Colt. 'Ain't no lower life form than back shooters.'

The man shrugged as he caught sight of his men waiting beside their horses out in the windy street. They had followed him a long way on the promise of sharing the bounty, but now it looked as if their prize had been stolen from under their noses by a half-pint girl wearing a star. Keeping these men together might prove harder than the long chase they had shared trying to catch up with Valko.

'I'm gonna wire the governor and see if he'll give me permission to take your prisoner, missy,' Everett said in a low, deliberate fashion.

Betty Jones watched as the man moved to the doorway before she spoke again.

'You better get on with it 'cos the mayor is intending hanging him tomorrow, Marshal.'

Pausing, the lawman swung around and gritted his teeth.

'If you would tell me where the telegraph office is?'

'You'll have to ride forty miles south-east of here to a town called Cable Creek if you wanna send a wire.' She moved toward the man blowing into her tin cup. 'We ain't got no telegraph office in Bear Claw. It's the mountains, you see. It's just too wild to rig up the poles.'

'Forty miles?' Everett fumed.

'Cable Creek,' she nodded.

The posse mounted one by one slowly and waited for their leader. Everett placed his left foot into his stirrup and hoisted himself on to his horse.

'Which way is south-east?' he asked her.

'Down the trail you came up and hang a left at the foot of the mountain.'

'Forty miles round trip?'

'Each way, Marshal.'

The riders pulled their reins hard and spurred their mounts into action. She watched as they headed out of Bear Claw as fast as their horses would take them. When they were out of sight she felt the sweat running down her spine as she closed the door behind her.

For a few moments she shook from head to toe. Jenks had been right when he said they would have to bluff their way through the day. The marshal had believed her every word. She wondered what he would do when he discovered there was no telegraph office in the town called Cable Creek.

In fact, there was no town called Cable Creek.

13

As the afternoon sun began to slip below the skyline, Bear Claw continued to tick along to the constant hammering of joiners building the gallows in the town square. Monte Scott had ensured there was plenty of lumber for the gallows and more than enough men to man-handle it off the wagons for the men with the giant long-tooth saws. There was going to be a hanging in Bear Claw even if the victim was already dead.

The two main buildings which towered arrogantly over the scene were the town hall and the equally grandiose bank. The citizens seemed to be enthralled by the sight of the solid wooden structure as it gradually took shape. This was no mere hanging device they were erecting, this was a vote-winning ploy conceived in the fertile mind of Monte Scott. There had never been a proper hanging in Bear Claw and the ruthless politician knew it.

Nothing excited the voters like a good neck-stretching if it was done properly. As mayor, Scott was giving them what they wanted. They would remember his name at the next election. He would be the man who strung-up the notorious Valko Kid. He had made sure a thousand flyers had been printed and distributed around the saloons and gold diggings. The town was already beginning to swell as miners and ranchers began to drift in for the show. They would spend money to see the spectacle and the longer he delayed the event, the richer the town would become.

Scott was watching from his office window with his council of lackeys beside him. His men would work through the night to complete their gruesome task, and he felt satisfied.

'What if the Kid dies before we can

lynch him?' a voice asked from beside the mayor.

'There'll be a hanging even if I have to carry a corpse up them gallows steps,' Scott spat.

Directly opposite the town hall, the bank was doing its usual thriving business as ore was being exchanged for hard cash by the visiting miners. Tonight, the bank would remain open all night just to ensure it took as much gold from the miners as possible. This was an event like the Fourth of July. This was a dozen Saturday nights rolled into one. Horace Brooks had no idea as he moved around his opulent bank this most profitable of afternoons would soon turn into a nightmare of unimaginable proportions.

As the street lamps were being lighted around the town, a lone rider dressed entirely in black upon a pale-grey mount was slowly moving through the densely crowded streets.

He was making his way toward the house he knew belonged to the wealthy banker. This was the man who had long been the shadow of the Valko Kid. He had returned to set his plan into operation.

Turning into the town square, his confusion at the hundreds of people choking the streets trebled as he found it almost impossible to find a clear route for his nervous horse. Reining in, the rider stared over the top of his raised bandanna at the men hammering as their massive wooden platform began to take shape, unmistakable to anyone who had ever seen one before.

A gallows?

The rider swallowed deeply while he tried to control his mount as the crowds forced their way past him. They were being drawn to the edifice of death like moths to a flame. It was as if he were invisible to these pitiful creatures. All they could see was the massive wooden joists being trimmed and raised.

Suddenly the rider felt uneasy. This had not been something he had taken account of. This cast a different light on his carefully planned crime.

Who were they hanging?

He jabbed his spurs into the flesh of the grey and forced it through the crowd and into a narrow alley. The sun had now disappeared and the streets were glowing with a golden light as the coal-oil lanterns began to replace the sunlight. Shadows stretched down the dark alley as the rider dismounted and held his reins tightly.

Standing at the corner of the alleyway, the man who had long masqueraded as the Valko Kid knew the bank was far too busy doing business with hundreds of miners for him to be able to get anywhere near the man called Horace Brooks. He would have to devise a new plan quickly.

Then his deathly eyes screwed up as he began to remember the layout of the town. Pulling the reins hard, he led the horse along the dark alley slowly into the shadows.

He knew this stinking lane traced its way between many buildings before ending up behind the sturdy house where Brooks lived with his wife.

Deeper and deeper he walked into the blackness dragging the grey behind him. He had found a place where the crowds would not follow or hinder him.

Stepping into a stirrup to raise himself above the height of the fence, the ruthless man saw the rear of the brick and stone house. Lowering himself back on to the ground he tied his reins to the fence before opening the tall gate and entering the yard.

It was a mere ten steps to the rear door of the house. Placing a gloved hand on to the handle he turned it and felt a sudden rush of excitement as the door opened easily. Pulling out one of his guns from its holster he slowly entered the house. He could smell the aroma of expensive perfume coming from a room bathed in lamplight before him. The sound of a woman singing softly to herself filled his ears as he crept closer to the room. Then he saw her clearly, seated with her back to the open doorway, unaware of who or what had invaded her home.

His eyes narrowed as he watched the back of her head covered in fine Irish lace. Raising the gun as if it were a club he stepped silently forward until he was directly above her.

He had thought of his revised plan.

As he brought the heavy weapon down violently, he began to laugh. It was the laugh of a creature no longer worthy of being described as a human being.

It was the laugh of a madman.

14

The Valko Kid stood readying himself for what lay ahead. Only fate or God knew what that might be. For years he had tried desperately to catch the nameless outlaw who had destroyed his life yet it had been like trying to capture smoke.

In all that time, Valko had never given up hope of one day clearing his name. Until this moment.

Maybe it was the wound in his shoulder which had soured his soul and created the doubts which filled his mind. Whatever it was, the Kid doubted ever finding peace again, where he might once more be free to walk streets like normal men and never fear becoming the target of back shooters.

A single low flame illuminated the sheriff's office allowing all three of its occupants to hide their faces from the knowing eyes of the others.

Standing silently beside the female who proudly wore a star and the old doctor, as they watched the main street growing ever darker, the time finally seemed to have arrived.

Betty Jones stared at the tall, square-jawed man. He had shaved off the whiskers which had covered his face for so many days, not through any vanity dwelling within him but to waste time. The afternoon had seemed an eternity as he had waited for the sun to set once more and allow him half a chance of escaping this town.

Few words had been spoken over the past hour between the trio of very different souls.

The old man had brought Valko a steak meal and a slice of pie in order to rebuild his strength. The Valko Kid had eaten his meal silently as if words might choke him.

He felt stronger now and once more tortured by the guilt only known to good men.

Once again he had allowed himself to fall for the charms of a beautiful female and it did not sit well in either his mind or his heart. He had tried for so long to remain above all his human feelings yet now he had betrayed another sweet woman by allowing himself to taste happiness.

Betty knew their time together was doomed, but had been drawn to the man without knowing why. He had a strange simplicity about him which no evil man could emulate. From the first moment she had set eyes upon the tall, slim man she had felt herself inextricably drawn to him.

The Valko Kid stood beside the window with his index finger on the shade giving himself a clear view of the long street. He knew he ought to be thanking these two very special people yet was unable to find words. Each time he tried to say something his throat dried up. Words seemed stuck within his mind as the sound of the clock echoed about them. What could he say anyway? His face was etched with sadness but the shadows veiled him from their eyes.

The knocking on the rear door of the sheriff's office made all three heads turn at once.

'That'll be Freddie,' Jenks said, getting up from his chair and moving toward the bolted door.

Valko flipped the safety loop off the Colt in his right holster and moved deeper into the shadows of the dark office. He knew these might be his last moments on earth if Jenks were wrong about whose knuckles had rapped on the rear door. Clutching the pistol, he felt the terror returning to him. Once again he had become the victim of his own fears, of which only a gunfighter had any knowledge.

*   *   *

Freddie, the livery man, had gone back to his stable after knocking on the rear door as instructed earlier by the doctor.

He had left the magnificent saddled white stallion tied up in the back alley next to the sheriff's office.

'Valko,' Jenks called into the dark office as he studied the large animal. 'Your horse is here, son.'

The Kid moved slowly into the alley and ran a hand over the neck of his faithful mount. Suddenly he felt as if there was a chance to get away from this town and the ceaseless sound of hammering which bounced off its buildings.

'You look rested, old friend,' Valko said quietly into the animal's ear.

'You must ride, Valko,' Jenks said, resting a hand on to the taller man's arm. 'Ride fast and true. Get as far away from here as this fine creature can take you.'

Valko checked the saddle girth as the figure of Betty Jones moved out of the office carrying his meagre possessions. Their eyes met for a brief moment before he reluctantly turned away from a face he felt unworthy of even seeing.

'Your hat and saddle-bags, Valko.' Her voice was like melted butter as the old doctor walked away from them back into the dark office.

Clearing his throat, Valko leaned on to his saddle as if trying to find strength, not physical strength but inner strength. The sort a man must find to do something he does not want to do.

'What'll they do to you and Jenks when they discover I'm gone, Betty?' His voice was quiet and muffled by the sleeve his face was buried into.

'I don't give a damn,' she replied, moving closer to him. 'As long as you get away safely.'

'I cannot find the words to . . . ' Her hand muffled his mouth and turned his head toward her.

'Valko?'

Slowly he turned his entire body towards her and stared at her. She looked beautiful even in the blue moonlight which bathed them both.

'You are . . . '

'Take these.' Betty forced the bags

and hat into his hands and stepped away from him into the blackness.

Placing the Stetson upon his head he tossed the bags behind the saddle cantle before tying the leather laces tightly. He felt his heart beating as he held on to his reins.

'You better go, Valko.' Her voice seemed to crack as she spoke from the darkness of the wall. 'The posse are bound to have found out there ain't no such place as Cable Creek by now and be heading back here.'

'You are one beautiful person, Betty,' the Kid managed to say, as he hesitated beside the large horse.

'Ride through this alley. It comes out near the town square, but if you cut up behind the bank, you'll have a clear trail over the mountain.' Betty Jones felt his strong fingers on her arm as she tried to enter the office.

Pulling her gently toward him, Valko wrapped his arms around her. Then he drew her up until their lips met and thanked her the only real way he knew how. As they kissed he could taste the salt of her tears tracing its way into their mouths.

Somehow he managed to release her and step into his stirrup quickly. Before she could say another word, he had ridden down the alley away from her.

Then she felt another man's arms around her. Jenks held her tightly as he had done the day she was born. She had cried then too, but not like she was crying now.

15

Horace Brooks looked up at the clerk from behind his massive carved oak desk. He had been checking his ledgers all day as they were continually being revised by his army of tellers and clerks. The miners were flooding into Bear Claw even faster than he had expected and his vaults were being swollen by their gold nuggets and dust. He was here to provide these hard-working men with a service and even if it took all night he was going to keep the doors of his bank open. Every transaction made him richer and he knew they were unaware of how much profit he had rigged into his system of charges.

'What?' Brooks grunted angrily, as if to even glance away from the pages would cost him money.

'There's a man out here saying he has urgent information for you, Mr

Brooks,' the feeble bank worker said.

Glancing at his wall clock the banker gave a deep sigh before waving a hand around in the cigar-smoke-filled air.

'I guess you had better show him in, Smith.'

Brooks was chewing on his fat Havana as he studied the figures in his ledger. He could hear the sound of his busy bank through the partition wall as the figure walked into the office and closed the door. Without looking up from the pages of neat columns of penmanship he grunted, 'Speak up. I'm busy.'

'I'm kinda busy too, Brooks.'

It was a voice which had a terrible foreboding in its acidic tones. It was the sort of voice which forced even the busiest of men to pause and look up. Brooks looked up and felt uneasy at what met his eyes.

'What do you want?'

The man moved around the office wearing his weapons on his hips without looking at the banker whilst

159

carrying his empty saddle-bags upon his shoulder. He seemed interested in all the expensive finery which Brooks surrounded himself but not the man himself.

'I was told you had some urgent message for me.' Brooks began to feel his collar cutting into his fleshy neck as he tried to twist his neck around to watch the strange man dressed entirely in black.

'They call me the Valko Kid, Brooks,' the man said from behind his bandanna. 'I guess you have heard of me.'

A look of puzzlement covered Brooks's face.

'The Valko Kid?'

The man rested a hip on the edge of the broad desk.

'Yep.'

Horace Brooks pulled a large handkerchief from his breast pocket and mopped his face.

'You escaped from the jail?'

Now it was the strange man's turn to stare in confusion down at the banker.

'You got me mixed up with some other varmint, Brooks.'

Brooks continued sweating profusely and nodded at the gunman who was stretching the black leather gloves over his hands until they were so tight he could see the outline of the outlaw's fingernails through them.

'What do you want, Valko?' he stammered.

'Money, Brooks. Lots of money.'

Brooks swallowed. 'I've two dozen men out there at this very moment and if I . . . '

The outlaw reached into his shirt pocket and withdrew a small diamond-encrusted pin. He placed it before the banker and waited for the reaction.

'That's my wife's pin,' he declared.

'Correct,' the man nodded. 'My boys are keeping her company right now and if you do as I tell you, she'll not be cut up or interfered with.'

All the colour seemed to drain from the banker's face as the true horror of the situation hit him.

'I'll give you anything, but please do not harm her.'

The outlaw dropped the saddle-bags on to the desk off his shoulder.

'Fill the bags with money. Paper money. Twenties and fifties will be fine.'

The banker stood and picked up the bags before moving to the door which led straight into the busy bank where a dozen tellers were still working. As his hand held on to the door handle the man's voice carved into his spine.

'If I don't get back to my boys in five minutes they'll kill your woman and ride out, Brooks,' it warned.

Brooks's face glanced at the man still sitting on the edge of his desk.

'I'll not raise the alarm.'

'Wise. Very wise.'

★ ★ ★

Betty Jones had more on her mind than being the sheriff of Bear Claw as she strolled with the elderly Jenks into the crowded town square. Her thoughts were on the outlaw she had allowed to escape and the mixed emotions his fleeing had brought. Now, more than ever, as she moved arm in arm with the medical man, she began to realize she had made the correct decision. The gruesome sight of the massive wooden gallows before the hundreds of spectators chilled her to the bone. Now as she stood upon the steps of the town hall staring at the men testing the trap she felt vindicated by her actions.

Flaming torches around the gallows added extra illumination to the sweating men as they continued their labours. The flickering light traced across the faces of the crowd. The look of eager anticipation was on every upturned face. These were not blood-thirsty people who gathered, these were faces showing all the instincts of a bygone time: they could smell the scent of the kill.

Betty held Jenks's arm tighter when she suddenly became aware the faces in the massive crowd belonged not only to men but women and children too.

'My God, Jenks,' she muttered.

'Exactly.' Jenks patted the back of her wrist with his hand as if he knew exactly what she was thinking about.

Before she could utter another word, her attention was captured by the sight of two men walking down the stone steps of the bank opposite, two men she thought she recognized.

'Is that who I think it is, Jenks?' Betty pointed at the distant figures.

Screwing his eyes up the old doctor bit his lip.

'If I didn't know better, I'd say that was Horace Brooks and Valko.'

'That's what I was thinking.' Betty Jones felt the fine hair on the nape of her neck tingling as she began to wonder whether or not they had been duped by the outlaw.

'Surely he would be long gone by now?' Jenks wondered aloud.

'Unless Valko figured he'd rob the bank before leaving Bear Claw,' she growled.

'It might be one of Brooks's men escorting him home, Betty.'

'Since when did old Horace require a bodyguard, Jenks?'

They looked at one another before moving back down to street level and heading in the general direction of the two men. Their task in getting across the square was hampered by the crowds. It seemed to swirl like a river as bodies swayed from one direction to the next. Somehow the pair made it to the sidewalk but they had lost sight of the two men.

'Where did they go?' Jenks asked, as he was pushed around by people heading in and out of stores and saloons.

The sheriff flicked the safety loop off her gun hammer and moved the old man against a wall.

'Stay here whilst I try and cut my way through this bunch of fools and catch up with them,' she said.

The doctor watched as she quickly vanished into the mass of swirling bodies clutching her six-gun. Jenks knew if Valko had deceived them, she would not be forgiving.

★   ★   ★

Valko reined in hard. He had allowed Snow to thunder away from Bear Claw and now the town was nothing more than a distant glow up in the mountain pass behind them. He was free and clear of the hangman's noose yet something had caused the Valko Kid to pull his magnificent stallion to a standstill.

Sitting astride the powerful animal, Valko glanced down at the small ranch below him. Even as the black rolling clouds masked the moon above their heads, the house seemed to attract his attention. For a moment the Kid just sat watching the building as if he could tell there was something very wrong within its walls. Although the trail ahead of him stretched into infinity and offered a sanctuary he had long sought,

Valko continued to look at the small ranch house below his vantage point.

Why the outlaw steered Snow down towards the crude structure even he failed to understand. The building appeared deserted but Valko felt something was wrong. The corral had a few horses moving freely around as if spooked by the strange moonlight or perhaps the approaching rider.

It was Snow who first noticed and shied away from the dark object a few feet away from the front of the building causing his master to stare hard at the dark ground. For a moment Valko did not recognize what his eyes were staring at.

Then he saw it was a body lying where it had fallen after being gunned down. Even in the darkness Valko could tell this had been a slaying and no mere accident. Dismounting, the young man strode over to the body lying covered in the frost of night. As the clouds passed by the face of the moon, the corpse seemed to sparkle. Valko tied his reins to the porch upright and stepped on to the creaking boards before gazing into the dark interior of the building. A single lamp lit up the faces of two women huddled together with eyes which had seen more horror than anyone could imagine.

The sobbing of the two terrified females caught him by surprise. He paused in the frame of the doorway afraid to venture further into their home. Afraid of what his presence might do to their fragile sanity.

'I ain't gonna hurt you ladies,' Valko whispered.

As the sound of his gentle voice filled their ears they suddenly realized this was not the other man who also dressed in dark clothing. This was not the crazed vermin who had torn away their underclothes and used them like they were of no value. This was a different man who stood respectfully waiting to be invited over their threshold. The mother and daughter collapsed on to the floor in total relief and began praying.

Valko removed his Stetson and waited. He found himself joining in their prayers for he, unlike them, had something to truly be thankful for. The Kid had no idea what he had ridden into but when they were ready they would tell him about the maniac who called himself the Valko Kid and how he had killed the man of the house in cold blood and then used both the females' bodies mercilessly for his own insatiable perversions. Not once, nor even twice, but continually like an animal unable to resist the weak and defenceless.

Leaving his Winchester and a box of cartridges with the two women, Valko stepped out into the cold night air, and turned his collar up against its icy chill. Listening to them sliding the wooden bolt across the door he untied the reins before stepping into his stirrup and hauling himself up into the saddle.

Sitting atop Snow, the Kid checked both his matched pearl-handled Colts were fully loaded before easing the mighty horse away from the wooden upright. Tapping his heels against the flanks of the white stallion he rode up the ridge before pausing. To his left a clear trail to freedom; to his right the glowing lights of Bear Claw rose into the night sky in the high mountain pass.

Valko turned the horse to his right and stood in his stirrups as he urged the stallion on. At first Snow seemed to realize they were returning to a place where there was nothing but danger waiting for its master, but soon responded to Valko's verbal encouragement.

With every stride of the huge horse, the Valko Kid drew closer to the town which was erecting a gallows in its town square just for him. His neck alone was required for its brand new noose.

He knew it was insanity to ride back towards Bear Claw but the man who had lived in the shadow of his name was there trying to rob the bank.

Valko had never been so close to this

maniac before. Maybe this might be his only chance at capturing him and proving his own innocence.

As Snow thundered across the frost-covered ground, Valko held on to the reins tightly. He knew every stride the mount took brought him closer to his own execution but it mattered not to him. All that mattered now was justice, and yet justice was something which had long ignored his own plight.

As he gritted his teeth, Valko allowed the horse to charge at the distant town. Thoughts of the two females back on the small ranch ate at his guts. He had never seen women so crazed with fear before. Nobody had the right to do that to anyone, but the man who delighted in calling himself 'Valko' had done so and more. How much more, the young outlaw might never know, not that he had any desire to know the true brutal details.

Wearing the darkness of night as his only shield, he rode on and on towards Bear Claw.

16

The muffled pistol shot could have come from anywhere. Betty Jones gripped her Colt .45 and swung around to look at the sea of bodies filling the town square. There were many guns and rifles raised into the air as excited people urged the workers to complete their task and finish the gallows. Concentrating hard, the sheriff knew it was none of those which had been fired. Taking another half-dozen steps along the boardwalk before pausing, Betty waited beneath the lamp outside Horace Brooks's splendid home.

Again the sound of a shot found her ears over the ranting of the frenzied crowd but this time she knew exactly where it had originated: the elegant home of Horace Brooks behind her. Pushing the gate open she rushed to the solid front door and hammered at it with the grip of her Colt. Another shot rang out from within the house causing her to step back. Wood splintered out above her head as the red-hot lead passed through the door.

For a moment she hesitated. Luckily for her she was far shorter than the average male sheriff. The top of the door split open once more as yet another deadly missile breached its highly painted surface.

Betty wiped the sawdust from her face and looked around the scene. She alone in the entire town knew there was someone firing bullets at her. The sheer volume of the crowd drowned out practically all other sound. Without waiting for another bullet to be fired through the door, she ran to the small picket fence and cleared it in one leap. Staring down into the dark alley she pulled the hammer back on her gun until it cocked and then began the long walk which led to the rear of this house and several other structures.

The agile female crouched down as

she came to the tall fencing she knew guarded the back of Horace Brooks's home. The alley was dark and no moonlight could penetrate its narrowness. Then she heard the sound of spurs and the snorting of a horse. Even in the pitch blackness of the alleyway she could tell the sound of a rider mounting a nervous animal.

Before she had time to stand fully upright, a horse drove into the sheriff sending her cart-wheeling backwards only pausing when faced with the impenetrable street full of excited people. Bathed in the eerie orange glow of street lamps and fiery blazing torches, the horse reared up and whinnied in confusion. Only then did the dazed Betty Jones see the image which had so long fooled an entire legion of law officers.

Unable to proceed into the street, the rider tugged at his reins and forced the terrified dapple grey around to face the kneeling sheriff.

'Take a good look, girlie,' the rider

snarled down at the shaking woman. 'Not many folks get to set eyes on the Valko Kid.'

'Valko?' Betty yelled, as she finally managed to get to her feet. She leaned against the solid wall which was the corner of the banker's home staring up at the rider. To the ill-informed this creature who sat arrogantly above her fitted the description of Valko, but it was not him. Her brain raced as she scanned the ground for her gun. He wore black and was careful to keep his bandanna raised high before his face to disguise his features from those who might get close. The horse was indeed pale but she had seen Valko's white stallion Snow close up and there was no comparison between the two animals. Rubbing the soil from her bruised face she suddenly knew this was the man the Kid had long sought in vain.

The rider dug his spurs into his animal and it stepped closer to her bathed in the satanic glow of the street illumination.

'So you're the Valko Kid?' Betty said, moving back away from the snorting horse.

'Yep. Now tell me why you are wearing a star.' The voice drifted over her like molasses seeping from a grocer's ladle.

Clearing her throat she tried to appear confident.

'I'm the sheriff, Valko.'

The rider began to laugh as he drew one of his guns and aimed it down at her.

'Then I've gotta plug you, girlie,' he snarled slowly as his horse edged ever closer.

'Valko don't wear spurs,' Betty said, as her eyes glanced behind her at the darkness of the winding alley.

The rider pulled his horse to a halt as if stunned by the statement.

'How would you know such a thing?' he raged.

'Because I've met the real Valko Kid,' Betty replied. 'He was in my jail until about an hour ago.'

The imposter dismounted quickly and grabbed her shirt front before pulling her close enough to feel the cold steel of his gun barrel pressing into her middle.

'Valko is here?' he growled in a half-hushed tone.

'Who do you think they are building the gallows for?'

The eyes which blazed over the bandanna glinted in the flickering lamplight. They were not the eyes of a man to toy with. They showed true fear as they darted from side to side.

'Where is he?'

'You sound scared, mister.'

'The gallows are for Valko, you say?'

'It seems you have arrived in time for your own hanging.' Betty felt his grip loosen as his crazed brain tried vainly to take in all the information she had given him. Finally he released her and gathered up his reins once more.

'You have the real Valko Kid in your jail,' he drawled as he mounted the grey.

Before she could reply, Betty's vision was blinded by the white flash and then the deafening sound of his gun. She felt the thud of the bullet as it impacted into her sending her falling into the black shadows. As she lay on her back in the mud her last sight was of the rider slowly passing above her into the blackness as he rode the horse deeper into the alley. Then it was as if a veil was covering her face, blurring everything until she felt herself falling into a terrifying whirlpool.

17

Jenks had somehow managed to reach the corner of the long street which edged the town square when he saw the flash of the familiar large white stallion coming around the corner of the small houses at the rear of the impressive bank. The rider dismounted and tied his reins securely to a hitching rail well away from the busy square before cautiously moving into the crowd.

The elderly doctor waved and caught Valko's attention then waited for the young man to reach him.

'What the heck are you doing here, Kid?'

Valko rubbed his chin as his eyes flashed about them.

'It's a long story.'

'Were you walking with the banker a few minutes ago, Kid?'

Valko pushed the brim of his Stetson

up off his face as he stood towering over the doctor.

'I just rode back into town, Jenks,' he replied. 'Where's Betty? I gotta find her and tell her something.'

'Betty went after the banker and a man dressed like you,' Jenks informed the outlaw who studied the ever-growing crowd.

'That's the one I've been after,' Valko said, as his eyes searched the crowd for a sign of the man.

'What the hell are you doing back here?' Jenks felt every hammer blow which echoed about the square from the joiners as they toiled at the final stages of their task. 'You should have been free and clear by now.'

'I was . . . ' Valko's voice faded as he stared at the gallows which now towered over the hundreds of eager souls.

'That's for you.'

'I figured.' Valko swallowed deeply.

'Why did you return?'

'I had two choices, Jenks,' Valko

sighed. 'I could have kept running or return to find the bastard who has been pretending to be me. This might be my only chance at catching my 'shadow'.'

'But this is suicide, boy.' Jenks held his friend's arm.

'Maybe.' Valko moved down the street with the older man at his side. 'Where did you see this banker and my shadow?'

'Near the bank,' retorted Jenks.

'Take me there. Maybe we can find out where they went and where Betty has gone.'

The lean younger man went where the doctor led him. Each step drew them deeper into the crowd of people who were oblivious to their very existence.

From the corner of the bank they headed across the street through the sea of excited bodies until they reached the exact point where Horace Brooks and the evil pretender had been spotted walking together.

Valko stood uneasy with his back to

the crowd of people as the old doctor rubbed his sweating head with a handkerchief.

'Where now?' Valko asked.

'I don't know.' Jenks shook his head. 'I lost sight of the pair when Betty and me came down off the steps of the town hall and entered this damn crowd.'

The Kid looked up and down the street anxiously.

'Where does this banker live?'

'Of course.' Jenks grabbed his friend's elbow and pulled him along the boardwalk to the corner before pointing at the stone and brick structure.

'Is that the banker's house?' Valko gave a surprised gasp at the sight of the large building.

'Yep.' Jenks pulled the young man along until they reached the picket fence.

Valko moved quickly to the front door before stopping when he saw the bullet holes which scarred its surface.

'Dear Lord.'

Jenks's hands wrestled with the brass door handle.

'It's bolted, Kid.'

The Valko Kid seldom felt anger but as he brushed the old doctor aside, a fury swelled up within him. A fury which gave him such inner strength, he somehow managed to kick the solid wooden door off its hinges with one well-placed strike of his right boot.

Entering low with both guns drawn and hammers cocked, Valko moved through the house with Jenks on his heels. As they moved into the ornate parlour, their eyes narrowed with the horror which met them. Even in the flickering lamplight neither man had seen such carnage.

Both Brooks and his wife lay dead in their own blood. The banker had two bullets well placed in his silk vest and lay lifeless at the feet of his seated wife. Her body was slumped like a rag doll where she had been clubbed to death. The floor seemed covered in blood which was already beginning to congeal. Whoever had done this had walked through the blood and left a trail of red footprints away from the scene.

Neither man spoke as they continued to follow the footprints of blood out into the hall and into the kitchen out into the dark rear yard.

Valko was first to reach the gate to the alley. Entering the alley both men stood in the unearthly darkness.

'What now?' Jenks whispered.

Valko raised his arm and pointed toward their right.

'Do you hear something?'

The old man followed as Valko carefully walked towards the strange sound. Sixteen paces along the alley led them into a twilight of street light which filtered down towards them. Then they saw the crumpled body lying motionless against the wall of Brooks's house.

Holstering his weapons, Valko knelt down and frantically rubbed the dirt from the face.

'Betty!' he exclaimed.

Jenks lifted her limp wrist and searched desperately for any sign of a pulse. Finally his fingertips located a faint vibration as her heart fought for life.

'She's alive, Valko.'

'He shot her, Jenks. The vermin shot her,' Valko said as he felt the staggered breath coming from her lips and the pitiful sound which she was making.

'There's a chance I can save her, if we can get her back to my office,' Jenks said feverishly. 'I gotta operate quick to get that bullet and stop this bleeding.'

Valko scooped the limp woman off the ground and raced behind the doctor out into the well-lit streets through the hordes who did not seem to notice their plight. They did not stop running until they had reached the doctor's small office.

18

United States Marshal Clem Everett
was now enraged as he led his band of
trail-weary men up the narrow tree-
lined draw into Bear Claw. They had
ridden close to ninety miles, full circle,
on a wild goose chase searching for a
town called Cable Creek before coming
to the unanimous decision they had
been hoodwinked by a mere slip of a
girl.

For the past ten miles they had
merely allowed their spent horses to
find their own pace. Now as they
passed between the first of Bear Claw's
street lamps the riders wondered why
the place seemed almost deserted.

Reining up outside the sheriff's
office, Everett sat and studied the area.
Along the entire main thoroughfare
only one building had light emanating
from behind its shades. Only the

doctor's office showed any sign of life. Even the saloons were locked up.

'Something's wrong,' Everett said across to his men who encircled his mount.

Josh Cavey raised himself up off his saddle and rubbed his sore groin.

'I gotta get me into a hot tub, Clem.'

Booth Dawson held his reins lightly in a gloved hand and listened to the sounds which were drifting on the night air.

'If I didn't know better, I'd say there is one heck of a party going on someplace close.'

His companions all began to nod as they too heard the sound of drunken revelry in the distance.

Everett gritted his teeth and turned his horse's head toward the sound and spurred.

'Let's go find us a party, boys,' he drawled.

As the posse began riding down the deserted street, a lone figure watched from an alley atop a dapple grey. The outlaw who had lived as the shadow of Valko watched and wondered who these men were. As they passed his hiding place he spotted the tin stars glinting in the light of the street lamps.

Nervously his fingers emptied his pistols of their used cartridges and replaced fresh shells into the still warm cavities of his revolver's chambers.

The posse had added a new dimension to his problem.

Fear was something this evil man had seldom experienced, but as the riders rode by, he felt sweat running down his face and soaking into his bandanna.

He knew these men had come from the desert plains. He was not prepared to take that route of escape. Somehow he had to find his way back to the trail he had used to enter Bear Claw. He knew the lands beyond the small ranch well. If he reached the ranch his knowledge of the wilderness would save him. Turning the grey around in the alley the outlaw rode into its darkness trying to recall the twisting route back

188

to the town square. To head back toward the scene of one of his atrocities was something he had never done before. Yet this was his only choice. As he rode the horse slowly through the maze of lanes he felt uneasy.

Somewhere in this town, the man he had impersonated for so many years, might be hiding. Lying in wait. Ready to seek vengeance.

The outlaw steered the horse on, rubbing the sweat from his brow every few seconds. Even from the vantage point of a high saddle, it was still almost impossible to see anything clearly.

* * *

'Bring the lamp closer, Valko,' Jenks said as he probed for the bullet with his razor-sharp scalpel.

The Kid leaned over the naked form of Betty Jones as she lay upon the flat slab in the rear of the doctor's office.

'Put a few more drops of chloroform on the mask and hold it to her face for a few seconds,' Jenks instructed. 'Then put the mask in that glass jar again. Otherwise you and me will be sleeping like babies too.'

Valko did as he was told. He had followed every command to the letter and yet felt as if he were responsible for her lying so close to death.

Then Jenks reached down carefully to the wound where his scalpel had been searching and pulled out the small chunk of lead.

'Got the bastard,' Jenks laughed as he tossed the blood-covered object into a tray at his side. Valko was placing the chloroform mask back into its safety jar when he heard the bullet rattling around in the white enamel tray.

'Is she gonna be OK now, Jenks?'

The clear eyes of the doctor looked straight at him for a fraction of a second before returning to his patient.

'If I can stop this damn bleeding.'

The Valko Kid stood across the table from the doctor and watched as the man worked so tirelessly. He had never seen such skill before and it made him wonder if he might ever achieve anything in his own life. Fleeing the ropes of one posse after another was no way to live. For years he had merely existed like an animal trying to avoid the hunters.

Caressing Betty's hair with the palm of his hand, Valko knew it was only a matter of hours until dawn. Once the sun rose, they would find where he had hidden Snow. Then they would find him.

He wondered if the killer with so much blood on his hands was still in Bear Claw. Yet the Valko Kid stood assisting the doctor, knowing every passing minute brought his own violent death closer.

Unlike other men in his situation, Valko would remain to help two people who had helped him. There were no choices.

★　★　★

Everett led his men into the Crazy Horse Saloon on the edge of the town square. They had found the party which was echoing around Bear Claw. None of the trail-sore riders were in the best of moods as they pushed the drunken souls from their way to the bar.

'Whiskey.' Everett slammed a fist on to the bar top. 'A bottle each.'

Tossing a few silver coins at the bartender, the marshal rested a boot on to the brass rail and stared into the long mirror at their bedraggled images.

'Where do you reckon they got the Valko Kid hid, Clem?' Cavey asked.

Swallowing the welcome refreshment Everett turned to face his men.

'I'm so dog tired, I don't give a hoot.'

'We gonna rest up here tonight?' Booth Dawson asked.

Everett returned his attention to his bottle and began pouring himself another three fingers of whiskey into a crystal tumbler when his attention was caught by a reflection in the long mirror behind the bartenders. He had seen an image which had filled his mind for years.

Spinning around Everett searched the windows until he caught sight of the dark-clothed rider on a grey mount passing before the crowd.

'Valko!' Everett exclaimed pointing at the rider until each and every one of his men had also spotted the slow-moving rider edging through the crowd of people who encircled the gallows.

Drawing their guns from their holsters the men all followed the brooding marshal out into the street.

'Valko!' Everett screamed at the rider.

The rider pulled up his mount and turned his head to stare back at the line of dusty lawmen. He had made it to the very heart of the crowd on his dapple grey and was now surrounded by men, women and children. Pulling both his Colts from their holsters, the outlaw began firing at Everett and his companions. Suddenly the entire area seemed to be filled with the screams of bewildered people who were caught in the middle of a shootout.

Clem Everett went down on one knee and began returning the lead which was coming at him. Dawson fell at his feet, as did Brad Carter before the remaining deputies spread out. As the smell of gunsmoke filled the night air, the crowd suddenly began to panic like a stampeding herd of long-horn steers.

People seemed to be running in all directions as bullets passed back and forth. The outlaw drove his spurs deep into the hide of his horse and began ploughing down all who surrounded him. One by one people fell beneath the hooves of his grey as he continued firing at the law officers. Riding the animal in a circle he seemed unable to miss his targets. Soon the bodies of hysterical people were littering the town square around the mighty wooden gallows.

Everett rolled over behind a water trough as he saw two more of his men falling wounded into the damp ground.

Reloading his guns the marshal lay on his side — watching the crazed figure riding down the crowd as if he were trying to build a wall of human bodies between himself and Everett.

Then the outlaw dismounted and holstered his guns. He tied his reins to one of the many blazing torches and pulled the Winchester from its scabbard. Cocking the repeating rifle he knelt and started firing.

It was as if the man's bullets knew exactly where the marshal was. Every one of the lethal projectiles seemed to pin Clem Everett behind the trough until he was unable to move a muscle.

Everett felt the water splashing over him from the trough, as he saw the last of his trusty followers being cut down by the vicious rifle shells of the man he thought was the Valko Kid.

The townspeople had now fled the square yet the screaming seemed even louder as it echoed around them.

Bullets tore away at the trough, causing the marshal to look around for better shelter. There seemed to be none.

Then he caught sight of the figure in the saloon windows moving closer to him. For the first time in all the years Everett had chased Valko, he had suddenly become the hunted and not the hunter.

'Brad? Booth? Josh?' Everett called out vainly as he stared across at his men lying around him. There were a few movements from one of the men but none seemed capable of replying.

He was alone.

19

The elderly physician stared at his young companion as he covered Betty Jones with a white sheet. She was now breathing normally.

'Something's happening, Jenks,' Valko said as he peered around the edge of the window shade.

'An old-fashioned, shootout by the sound of it, Kid,' Jenks nodded as he poured the fresh water into a bowl and began scrubbing the blood off his hands.

'It must be him,' Valko growled.

'The rat who likes telling folks he's you?'

Valko nodded.

'What can you do?' Jenks scrubbed his nails with a well-soaped brush.

The Kid walked across to the pale beauty who lay sleeping on the table.

'I can try and catch the varmint.'

Jenks shrugged as he moved to a rail and pulled a fresh towel into his wet hands.

'And then?'

Valko's face seemed troubled as he stared down at Betty.

'If I catch the man I can drag him into the jail and maybe folks will believe me.'

Jenks walked to the tall man and looked up into his face.

'I'll make sure they listen, Kid.'

'What about Betty?'

'Go. Now only God can decide her fate. I've done all I can.'

Reluctantly, Valko strode across the office and picked up his belt and strapped it around his middle. Checking the two matched Colts, he placed his Stetson on his head and grabbed the door handle. For a brief moment he paused, then without looking back he opened the door and stepped out on to the boardwalk before pulling it shut behind him.

Dozens of people were running

frantically along the street away from the sound of the gunfire. Pulling the brim of his black hat down over his temple, Valko began to race toward the noise.

★ ★ ★

The sight which met the eyes of the Valko Kid chilled his blood as he rounded the corner and entered the town square. The number of bodies strewn around the area was incalculable and the sounds of wounded women, and even children, filled the cold night air.

For a moment, he did not see anything except the massive wooden gallows which was surrounded by tall blazing torches. On the far side of the structure he spotted the dapple grey tethered to one of the torches. Then bullets lit up the square. Rifle bullets.

Drawing both his Colts, Valko swung about on his high heeled boots and saw the man clutching the

199

Winchester at hip level.

The outlaw dressed entirely in black was standing directly above a cowering man who had sought refuge behind a water trough.

'I'm the Valko Kid and you're gonna die,' the chillingly familiar voice screamed down at his human target.

'No, Valko. No,' the voice of Clem Everett pleaded.

'He ain't the Valko Kid. I am.' Valko raised his right-hand pistol and pulled the hammer back with his thumb and aimed directly at the man. He had the swine in his sights as he focused down his arm and along the gleaming Colt .45.

Then he moved his aim to the rifle stock and squeezed his trigger.

The crazed outlaw who relished in pretending to be the Valko Kid stood shocked as his carbine was torn from his grip by the accuracy of the one man he did not wish to meet.

Clem Everett gazed bewildered at the two men both proclaiming to be Valko.

For once in his life he had cause to be grateful to at least one man calling himself Valko.

Valko moved towards the figure who swiftly drew and fired both his weapons. The Kid felt his outheld pistol being ripped from his hand and the burning sensation in his right wrist.

Throwing himself on to his belly, Valko rolled over several times until he found himself beneath the gallows. Looking at his painful wrist he saw the deep graze and the blood beginning to seep from his ruptured flesh. The pain was so intense he found his fingers numb.

From his vantage point he could see the long legs of his 'shadow' running towards his horse still firing at the trapped man and the wooden gallows.

Pulling his hammer back on his left-hand pistol, the Kid crawled out and raced at the running man. Flying through the air, he caught the man around his middle and brought him crashing down beside the waiting horse.

The snarling imposter lost both his guns as they struck the ground. Clenching both fists, he struck Valko hard with a left to the jaw and then a right to the temple. Stunned, the Kid rolled off his prey and found the man getting to his feet first. The boot which came thundering into Valko's middle sent him rolling over against one of the tall wooden torches. It fell down on to the massive gallows spilling its blazing coal tar soaked rags over the edifice.

Valko raised the pistol and then noticed his opponent was unarmed. Casting his gun aside, the Kid dragged himself up and grabbed the man. As they wrestled in the light of the gallows as it began to catch aflame, Valko stared directly into the man's eyes.

It was the same twisted man he had met all those years earlier.

Valko felt his right hand weaken as they grappled each other across the ground littered with innocent victims and fell into the flames.

Striking yet another solid blow to

Valko's chin, the imposter attempted to scramble free. As the fire raged around them, they fought their way up the steps to the top of the lethal wooden gallows. Blow for blow they stood striking out at one another. Valko seemed to take two punches for every single one he landed. His hand was now swollen and felt heavy as the man took full advantage. Then another kick hit Valko in his ribs and he staggered winded to the edge of the platform. Another hefty two-fisted blow across his neck sent Valko flying out into mid-air.

Hitting the ground, Valko lay watching as the man stood amid the flames above him. Burning embers began showering down over the stricken Kid forcing him to once more scramble to his feet.

Then the menacing outlaw leapt down from the platform as it was totally engulfed in flames. Valko staggered around the inferno and spotted his evil double picking up his guns and untying his horse before mounting.

Valko rushed around the massive bonfire toward the mounted man before seeing him raising one of his pistols. Diving beneath the legs of the dapple grey, he heard the shot blasting above.

The horse began to buck and kick out as the Kid tried to stay beneath the cinch strap of his mortal enemy. Bullets tore up the ground around him as the horse finally caught Valko with his hooves.

Dazed, Valko fell away from the horse.

As his eyes cleared, Valko saw the face of the man above him in the saddle of the grey. Raising both guns and aiming down at the helpless Kid, the imposter smiled. It was the same twisted smile dozens of other victims had witnessed over the years.

Valko glanced around for his own guns but could not see either of them. Then he focused on the two fingers as they squeezed the triggers.

Both hammers fell on empty chambers.

The look of total shock traced across the features of the rider as he continued squeezing his triggers. His guns were empty.

Valko somehow got back to his feet as the rider dragged his reins hard and spurred his mount. The horse thundered away from the scene of carnage out into the darkness. Valko staggered around the area until he found both his pistols. Suddenly as he limped along the street towards where he had left his faithful mount he came face to face with the figure of Clem Everett.

Both men stared hard at one another.

'You saved my life,' the marshal drawled.

Valko steadied himself.

'He had the bead on you.'

'He said he was Valko and so did you.' Everett picked up the Kid's Stetson and handed it to him.

Valko continued staggering along the silent street which still had the smell of gunpowder hanging in the air. The marshal kept pace with the outlaw.

'I don't understand,' Everett said as they turned the corner.

Valko pointed to the hitching rail and the magnificent white stallion which awaited him. The lawman stopped and watched as Valko untied the reins with his left hand and led the horse away from the rail. Valko stepped into his stirrup and hauled himself up on to the back of his mighty horse where he sat trying to conceal his injuries.

'You are the Valko Kid,' Clem Everett said, still trying to understand.

'And you are Clem Everett,' the Kid tried to smile through his bruises. 'United States Marshal.'

Both men looked at one another — seeking answers to questions unsaid.

Finale

Betty Jones's long lashes fluttered as she awoke to see the bruised and battered face of Valko hovering above her.

'Valko?' Raising her hand, Betty gently touched his jaw as if confused by his appearance.

'Jenks is a pretty good surgeon.' His words were softly spoken as he held her small fingers in his own injured right hand.

'I thought you had returned until I got close to the . . .'

Valko touched her lips with his own then tucked her arm beneath the sheet once more.

'I've gotta go catch me an outlaw calling himself the Valko Kid, Betty.'

Turning her head, she watched as he slowly limped towards the door of Jenks's office.

'You're hurt, Valko.'

His face looked back at her as he held the door handle.

'Kinda.'

Opening the door, Valko stepped out on to the boardwalk and eased the door shut behind him. It was nearly dawn and the stars were beginning to fade above the town of Bear Claw. Jenks sat next to the hitching rail sipping at a cup of cold coffee whilst the white stallion patiently awaited its master.

As Valko hobbled to the edge of the boardwalk, the doctor rose to his feet and rested an arm around the gunfighter.

'You're busted up, Kid. Let me tend them injuries.'

It was a strange smile which greeted the older man's concern as Valko stepped into his stirrup and threw his leg over the large animal. Gathering up the reins he sat trying to disguise his pain from the man.

'Betty requires every ounce of your skills. Not me.'

The figure of Clem Everett stepped out from the shadows opposite and stood watching as the Kid turned his mighty stallion and rode slowly towards him. Briefly pausing above the marshal, he looked down and spoke.

'Figuring on getting another posse together, Marshal?'

'Maybe. When I've buried my dead,' replied Everett.

Valko nodded.

'Who was that *hombre* you fought with, Valko?'

'My evil shadow?' Valko shrugged.

'Then who have I been hunting all these years, Kid?'

'The wrong man.' Valko tapped his boots and the stallion began to move once more.

As the white horse found its stride, Valko raised an arm and headed quickly through the still smouldering square and out of Bear Claw.

Everett looked at Jenks who was

standing next to the door of his office. Both men nodded to one another and yet did not speak.

As the sun finally rose over the town set between two mountain peaks, the Valko Kid was gone.

We do hope that you have enjoyed reading this large print book.

Did you know that all of our titles are available for purchase?

We publish a wide range of high quality large print books including:
Romances, Mysteries, Classics
General Fiction
Non Fiction and Westerns

Special interest titles available in large print are:
The Little Oxford Dictionary
Music Book, Song Book
Hymn Book, Service Book

Also available from us courtesy of Oxford University Press:
Young Readers' Dictionary
(large print edition)
Young Readers' Thesaurus
(large print edition)

For further information or a free brochure, please contact us at:
Ulverscroft Large Print Books Ltd.,
The Green, Bradgate Road, Anstey,
Leicester, LE7 7FU, England.
Tel: (00 44) **0116 236 4325**
Fax: (00 44) **0116 234 0205**

GUNS OF THE GAMBLER

M. Duggan

Destitute gambler Ben Crow arrives in Mallory keen to claim his inheritance, only to discover that rancher Edward Bacon has other ideas. Set up by Miss Dorothy, who had fooled him completely, Ben finds himself dangling on the end of a rope. Saved from death, Ben sets off in pursuit of Miss Dorothy, determined upon retribution. However, his quest for vengeance turns into a rescue mission when she is kidnapped by a crazy man-burning bandit.

SIDEWINDER

John Dyson

All Flynn wants is to be Marshal of Tucson, but he is framed by the territory's richest rancher, Frank Buchanan, and thrown into Yuma prison. Five years later Flynn comes out, intent on clearing his name and burning for vengeance. Fists thud, knives flash and bullets fly as he rides both sides of the law and participates in kidnapping and double-dealing. He is once again arrested for a murder of which he is innocent. Can he escape the noose a second time?

THE BLOODING OF JETHRO

Frank Fields

When Jethro Smith's family is murdered by outlaws, vengeance is the one thing on his mind. He meets the brother of one of the murderers, who attempts to exploit Jethro's grudge in the pursuit of his own vendetta. The local preacher, formerly a sheriff, teaches Jethro how to use a gun. With his new-found skills, Jethro and his somewhat unwelcome friend pit themselves against seemingly impossible odds. Whatever the outcome lead would surely fly.

SEVEN HELLS AND A SIXGUN

Jack Greer

Jim Cayman had been warned about Daphne Rankin, his boss's wife, and her little ways. When Daphne made a play for Jim and he resisted, the result was painful and about what he had feared. But suddenly matters went beyond the expected and he found himself left to die an awful death. Only then did he realise that there was far more than a woman scorned. He vowed that if he could escape from the hell-hole he would surely solve the mystery — and settle some scores.